Indy realized what this treachery was all about. "That's what you've got these slaves digging for...these children..." The anger started to churn within him again.

"They dig for gems to support our cause," Mola Ram assented, "and yes—they also search for the last two stones. Soon we will have all five Sankara Stones, and then the Thuggee will be all-powerful."

"Can't accuse you of having a vivid imagination..." Indiana jibed.

"You do not believe me," the High Priest focused on Indy now. "You will, Dr. Jones. You will become a *true* believer."

Starring

Harrison
Ford

Kate
Capshaw

Amrish
Puri

Roshan
Seth

Phillip
Stone

and Ke Huy Quan

Directed by
Steven Spielberg

Produced by
Robert Watts

Screenplay by
Gloria Katz &
Willard Huyck

Associate Producer
Kathleen Kennedy

Executive Producers
Frank Marshall and
George Lucas

Story by
George Lucas

Music by
John Williams

A Lucasfilm Ltd. Production
A Paramount Picture

INDIANA JONES
and the
TEMPLE OF DOOM™

by James Kahn

*Screenplay by Gloria Katz
& Willard Huyck
Story by George Lucas*

BALLANTINE BOOKS ● **NEW YORK**

Library of Congress Catalog Card Number: 84-90855

ISBN 0-345-31457-3

Cover art and insert supplied by Lucasfilm Ltd. (LFL)

Printed in Canada

First Edition: June 1984

1

Out of the Frying Pan...

Shanghai, 1935

The nightclub had that wild and smoky air. Ladies and gentlemen and not so gentle men, of every
nationality, and some no nation would claim, sat,
formally attired, at tables that were scattered around
the dance floor. Cigarette girls with long legs, boun-
cers with long faces, exotic food, tuxedoed waiters,
laughter soft and loud, champagne and broken
promises and opium lacing some of the tobacco—
that was the flavor to the smoke. A decadent place,
in a time of deep decay. But still, *très gai*. Like the
last party before the apocalypse. In a few years the
world would be at war.

Along the side wall, Deco curves and Oriental
arches weaved around to form private booths, or
step-up balconies. The bar was off to the back. Up
front, beside the kitchen doors, stood the bandstand, slightly raised, and beside it, directly before
the dance floor, was the stage.

Flanking the stage were two giant, carved wooden statues: Chinese warlords slouching on their thrones, sporting golden broadswords, smiling coolly, as if presiding over these festivities.

Beside the stage-left statue, an enormous gong hung by two thick cords, from the ceiling almost to the floor. In bas-relief on its face, an angry dragon hovered above a great mountain. Beside the gong stood a muscular attendant in harem pants, the striker resting across his bare chest.

Facing front, center stage, its mouth open wide, was the head of a huge dragon. Its great eyes bulged frantically in different directions, its *papier-mâché* antennae quivered in uneasy resonance with the clatter of the room, its paper-lantern scales rippled back to the curtains.

And now smoke began to issue from its maw.

Ceremoniously, the attendant struck the gong.

Fire-red light suffused the steam filling the dragon's mouth. The smoky light poured down the steps, off the stage, onto the dance floor, as the band began playing.

And then, slowly, through the jaws of the beast, out of its fiery snarl, emerged the woman.

She was twenty, maybe twenty-five. Green-blue eyes, dark blond hair. She wore a high-necked, fitted gold-and-red sequinned gown, with matching gloves, spike heels, butterfly earrings. She paused at the dragon's lip, reached overhead to tug coyly on one of its upper teeth, then stepped forward with a sultry purr. Her name was Willie Scott. She was a knockout.

A dozen girls danced down the stairs that winged the dragon's head. They fluttered fans before their exquisitely painted faces; they wore thigh-length golden kimonos, showing more than a glimpse of silk stocking, as Willie started to sing:

> "Yi wang si-i wa ye kan dao
> Xin li bian yao la jing bao jin tian zhi
> Dao
> Anything goes."

The crowd was mostly inattentive, but Willie mostly didn't care. She went through her moves like a pro, up the steps and down, growling her song, while her mind wandered in the smoke that swirled over the stage, floating thickest around the set-creature's head, like the dreams of the dragon. In her mind, this was no sleazy Shanghai night-spot: it was a Grand Stage. And these two-bit hoofers behind her were a tight chorus line, and it was back in the States, and she was the glamorous star, rich and adored and dazzling and independent and...

The smoke cleared a little. Willie remembered where she really was.

Too bad for this mob, she thought. *They're too low down to appreciate a class act when it taps right up to their table.*

The bandleader cued her, and she went into her last chorus, pulling out a red scarf, taunting the audience from behind it.

"Anything goes!"

The band wrapped it up; the crowd applauded. Willie bowed. The three men at the front table clapped politely, managing to turn their lips up without smiling: the gangster Lao Che, and his two sons.

Vile scoundrels, dressed in the faintest veneer of *beau monde*.

3

Willie winked at them.

Or, more specifically, at Lao Che, who was currently her mealticket.

He nodded back at her—but then something else caught his eye, and a shadow held his face. As Willie ran back upstairs and offstage, she followed Lao Che's gaze, to see what it was that engendered his disfavor.

It was a man, entering the club, walking down the staircase at the back of the room. He wore a white dinner jacket with a red carnation in the lapel, black pants, vest, bow tie, shoes. Willie couldn't see much more than that, except that the man seemed to carry himself pretty well. He gave her a bad feeling, though. She wondered if he was some kind of cop.

She saw him reach the bottom of the stairs, where he was greeted by a waiter, just as she made her exit off stage. Her last thought on the matter was: *Well, he's pretty, but he looks like trouble.*

Indiana Jones stepped off the elevator and walked down the stairway into the Club Obi Wan just as the floor show was ending. He watched the twelve red-and-gold-clad dancers scurry out of sight to loud applause, smiled to himself: *Hey, don't run off now, ladies, I just got here.*

Nonchalantly, he finished descending the stairs, but his eyes scanned the room like a chary cat.

It was as he remembered it, only more so: the dissolute horde, the hollow revelry; these were the people of a dying tribe. He wondered if even their artifacts would last, if his own counterpart, in a thousand years, could dig up their boxes and jewelry and picture the life in this room. *Picture the lowlife, that is*, he thought, his eyes coming to rest on Lao Che's table.

When he reached the bottom of the stairs, a waiter came up to him. The man was young, though his hairline was thinning; slight of build, though there was something dangerous about him; half-Chinese, half-Dutch. His name was Wu Han.

He bowed slightly to Indiana, with a vacant smile of greeting, and spoke so that only Jones heard: "Be careful."

Indy nodded back absently, then walked toward Lao Che's group. They reseated themselves as he approached. The applause ended.

"Dr. Jones," said Lao Che.

"Lao Che," said Indiana Jones.

Lao was pushing fifty. Several layers of high living puffed out his cheeks and belly, but it was all hard under the surface. Like lizard meat. He wore a black silk brocade dinner jacket, black shirt, white tie. His eyes were heavily lidded, reptilian. On his left little finger he wore the gilt signet ring of the royal family of the Chang Dynasty—Indy noted this with professional admiration.

To Lao Che's left was his son, Kao Kan, a younger version of the old man: stocky, impassive, ruthless. On Lao's right sat his other son, Chen. Chen was tall, thin almost to the point of ghostliness. The white scarf hanging loosely around his neck made Indy think of the tattered swathing that sometimes clung to long-shriveled corpses.

Lao smiled at Indy. "Nee chin lie how ma?"

Chen and Kao Kan laughed malignantly.

Indy smiled in return. "Wah jung how, nee nah? Wah hwey hung jung chee jah loonee kao soo wah

5

shu shu." He turned the joke around on Lao Che.

The three seated men became silent. Lao stared at Indy with venom. "You never told me you spoke my language, Dr. Jones."

"I don't like to show off," Indy deadpanned.

Two bodyguards appeared, frisked him quickly, and faded out of sight again. He didn't like that, but he'd expected it. He sat down across from Lao.

A waiter arrived at the table with a large dish of caviar and a bucket of chilled champagne, which he set beside Lao.

The smile returned to the crime-lord's face. "For this special occasion I have ordered champagne and caviar." He stared at Indy with a strange intensity as he went on. "So it is true, Dr. Jones: you found Nurhachi."

Indy leaned forward slightly. "You *know* I did. Last night one of your boys tried to take Nurhachi without paying for him."

Kao Kan brought his left hand up and rested it on the table. It was newly bandaged. It was newly missing an index finger.

Lao Che seethed, nodding. "You have insulted my son."

Indy sat back. "No, you have insulted me. But I spared his life."

Lao gazed at Indy like a cobra at a mongoose. "Dr. Jones, I want Nurhachi." He placed a wad of bills on the lazy Susan that occupied the center of the table, and spun it around until the money rested in front of Indy.

Indy put his hand down on the pile, felt the thickness of the wad, converted his estimate to dollars, came up short. Way short. He revolved the turntable back to Lao, and shook his head. "This doesn't even begin to cover my expenses, Lao. I thought I was dealing with an honest crook."

Kao Kan and Chen swore angrily in Chinese. Chen half-stood.

Suddenly an elegant, gloved hand rested on Lao's shoulder. Indy let his eyes glide up the smooth arm to the face of the woman standing behind Lao; she stared directly back at Indy. "Aren't you going to introduce us?" she said softly.

Lao Che waved Chen back down to his seat. "Dr. Jones, this is Willie Scott," said Lao. "Willie, this is Indiana Jones, the famous archaeologist."

Willie walked around toward Indy as he rose to greet her. In the moment of the handshake, they appraised each other.

He liked her face. It had a natural beauty weathered by natural disasters, like a raw gem after a flood, crystal-rough and waiting for a setting. She wore a diaphanous butterfly barrette that seemed to grow out of the substance of her hair; Indy took this to indicate a certain extravagance to her personality, if not actual flightiness. She wore gloves; Indy saw this as a statement on her part: "I do a lot of handling, but I don't touch." She wore expensive perfume, and a sequinned dress cut high in front and low—real low—in back; Indy took this to mean she came on cool, and left you with a nice memory. She was with Lao Che. To Indy, this signaled alarm.

Willie saw at once this was the guy she'd noticed coming in at the end of her act. Her initial impression of him was even stronger now: good-looking, but so out of place the air was practically shattering around the table. She couldn't figure his place,

7

though. Archaeologist? That didn't wash. He had an interesting scar across his chin; she wondered how he'd got it. She was a connoisseur of interesting scars. And he sure had nice eyes, although she couldn't quite figure out the color. Sort of green-hazel-gray-sky-with-gold-flecks. Clear and hard and finally unreadable. Too bad, really. Any way you sliced it, he looked like seven miles of bad road.

She let her stare drift from his interesting scar to his unhazel eyes. "I thought archaeologists were funny little men always looking for their mommies," she teased.

"Mummies," he corrected.

They sat down.

Lao interrupted their brief conversation. "Dr. Jones found Nurhachi for me and is about to deliver him...now."

Indy was about to reply when he first felt, and then saw, the small round mouth of Kao Kan's gun pointing at him, waiting to speak. Indy didn't want to hear what the pistol had to say, though, so he grabbed a two-pronged carving fork from a nearby trolley as Willie was talking.

"Say, who's Nurhachi?" she asked innocently, still unaware of the imminent explosion.

In the next moment, she became aware. Indiana pulled her close, and held the fork to her side.

Willie held her breath a moment. To herself she said, *I knew it I knew it I knew it.* To Lao she said softly but urgently, "Lao, he's got a fork on me."

Indy spoke in monotone to Kao Kan. "Put the gun away, sonny." He increased the pressure with his weapon.

Willie felt the prongs dent her skin. She strove

to keep the fear out of her voice. "Lao, he's got a fork in me." She didn't think he'd actually use it, but you could never tell with men and their toys.

Lao Che gave his son a look; the boy put the gun down.

Indy pressed. "Now I suggest you give me what you owe me, or . . . anything goes." Then, to Willie: "Don't you agree?"

"Yes," she whispered icily.

"Tell *him*," Indy suggested.

"Pay the man," she told Lao.

Without saying a word, Lao took a small pouch from his pocket, put it on the turntable, sent it around to Indy and Willie. Indy motioned to her with his head; she picked up the sack and emptied a handful of gold coins out onto the table.

Indy was stone-faced. "The diamond, Lao. The deal was for the diamond."

Lao smiled, shrugged defeat, took a squat silver box from his vest pocket, put it on the turntable.

In the moment that Indiana's eyes were focused on the box, Kao Kan tipped a tiny bottle of white powder into the champagne glass beside him. And as the turntable passed him on its way to Indy, Kao Kan set the glass down on it, next to the coins and the silver box.

When the cache arrived before them, Willie opened the box. Inside was a hefty yet delicate diamond. "Oh, Lao," she breathed.

Diamonds were her delight and howling demon. They were hard, but brilliantly lovely. They were clear; they held every color. They were the magical reflection of her very self. And yet they were eminently practical: a diamond like this could make her rich, and blessedly independent from jerks like the yo-yos at this table.

Indy stabbed the fork into the table and picked up the jewel, pushing Willie away on her chair, back to her original position. She stared at him frostily. "You're a real snake." She'd finally placed the color of his eyes.

He ignored her to examine the gemstone. Perfectly cut, each facet representing a different plane of the ancient universe: unflawed, unmarred, unyellow. The university had been hunting a long time for this little bauble.

"Now," hissed Lao Che. "Bring me Nurhachi."

Indy waved to Wu Han, the waiter who'd originally met him at the entrance of the club. Wu Han came forward, a linen napkin draped over his left arm, a tray balanced on his right. In the center of the tray stood a small jade casket.

Willie's sense of intrigue was beginning to overcome her anger. Money, coins, jewels, threats . . . and now this exquisite miniature. "Who on earth *is* this Nurhachi?" she demanded.

Indy removed the small casket from Wu Han's tray, set it on the turntable, rotated it toward Lao Che. "Here," he smiled. "Here he is."

Willie watched it pass her on its way to Lao Che. "Must be kind of a small guy," she muttered.

Lao pulled the canister before him. His sons leaned close. Lao spoke quietly, reverentially, almost to himself. "Inside this sacred coffin are the remains of Nurhachi, the first Emperor of the Manchu Dynasty."

Indy picked up the champagne glass beside him and lifted it magnanimously in toast. "Welcome home, old boy." He drank.

Ashes? Willie thought. *That's the big deal? Ashes?* As far as she was concerned, there was no percentage in dwelling over things past. Present and future were the only tenses that mattered. The rest was supremely boring at best. She began to make up her face.

Lao grinned sharply at Indy. "And now, you will give me back the diamond."

The room felt like it was getting a bit warm to Indy. He pulled his collar away from his throat. "Are you developing a rare sense of humor, or am I going deaf?"

Lao held up a small blue vial.

That caught Willie's eye. *More treasures?* she wondered. "What's that?"

"Antidote," snapped Lao.

"Antidote to what?" Indy asked suspiciously. He suddenly had a premonition.

"To the poison you just drank," Lao sneered.

Willie got that worried feeling in her gut, that hell-in-a-handbasket feeling. "Poison!" she rasped. "Lao, what are you doing? I *work* in this place." But not for long, that feeling told her.

Indy put a finger into his champagne and rubbed the glass: a gritty residue coated the bottom.

"The poison works fast, Dr. Jones," Lao cackled.

Indy put the diamond on the table; held out his hand. "C'mon, Lao."

Chen picked up the diamond, stared into its glittering depth, smirked with satisfaction, put it back down, rotated the turntable toward his father. On its way past Willie, *she* picked it off the tray to study it. She'd never held a diamond this large before. This perfect. It almost hummed in her hand.

Lao had lost interest in the stone, though; he was

11

still fixated on the casket before him. "At last, I have the ashes of my honored ancestor."

Indy was getting more than impatient. Yellow spots were starting to dance in his vision. "The antidote, Lao." Lao ignored him.

This wasn't going right. Jones felt shaky, felt his options slipping away. In a flash, he grabbed the fork off the table and held it once more to Willie's ribs. "Lao," he rumbled.

"Lao," she echoed.

Lao Che, Kao Kan, and Chen only laughed. "You keep the girl," said Lao. "I find another one."

Willie stared at Lao as if she were just now understanding something she'd really known all along. "You miserable little hood," she said.

Wu Han suddenly stepped forward. "Please," he smiled at Lao. They all turned to see, under the tray on his arm, concealed from the restaurant at large, a gun. Pointing directly at Lao Che.

"Good service here," said Indy.

"That's no waiter," Willie suddenly realized. The fork was still in her side. Everyone was edgy; she didn't know which way to jump.

"Wu Han's an old friend," murmured Indiana. "The game's not up yet, Lao. The antidote."

As Indy reached out his hand, there was a loud POP at the next table. They all turned to look; a sodden American had just opened a bottle of champagne, and the foam was spraying over his two giggling lady companions. Waiters there opened more bottles; more loud reports, more spray, more laughter.

Indy returned his attention to his own table. He was feeling increasingly queasy, while next to him, he noticed, Wu Han was looking positively pale. "Wu Han, what is it—" he began—but before he could finish, Wu Han collapsed to the table.

It was only then that Indy saw the smoking gun in Chen's hand withdrawing under a napkin.

"Indy!" gasped Wu Han.

As Wu Han fell forward, Indiana stood, grabbed him, and lowered the wounded comrade into his own chair. "Don't worry, Wu Han," he whispered. "I'm going to get you out of here."

"Not this time, Indy," the dying man choked. "I followed you on many adventures, but now, into the great unknown mystery I go first."

And so he died.

Indy laid his friend's head down on the table. He felt flushed, sweaty.

Lao could hardly contain his glee. "Don't be so sad, Dr. Jones. You will soon join him."

Indy's legs suddenly became quite rubbery, and he staggered backwards.

Kao Kan chuckled. "Too much to drink, Dr. Jones?"

Indy stumbled back farther, colliding with the drunk at the next table. Even the deathly gaunt Chen smiled to see their startled faces peering dizzily at each other. In a rage, Jones pushed the drunk away, bumping into another waiter who was serving the adjoining table from a trolley—serving liqueur-soaked flaming pigeons on a skewer. Indy thought: *If nothing else, I'm gonna wipe that smile off Chen's filthy face.* In a single motion, he grabbed the flaming pigeon skewer, whirled around, hurled it at Chen.

The skewer buried itself to the fiery-pigeon-hilt in Chen's chest.

13

There was this long, suspended moment: the crowd's din hushed, suddenly vaguely aware of its own impending convulsion; the people surrounding Lao's table froze, like a held breath, poised on the vision of this wraithlike Chinese man in a dinner jacket, impaled on a silver spear, flaming birds casting his startled face in a queer and morbid light.

Then everything happened at once.

Willie screamed reflexively. The woman at the next table, seeing the matched skewer of Pigeon Flambé on the trolley beside her and, perhaps wondering who was next in line to get spiked, likewise shrieked. The rest of the restaurant exploded in chaos. Shouts, breaking glass, running, confusion...like the inside of Pandora's Box before the lid was removed.

Indy dove across the table to grab the small blue tube of antidote, but it skittered over the glassy surface, off onto the floor. Indy found himself face to face with Lao. He grabbed the vile gangster by the lapels and snarled hoarsely at him: "Hoe why geh faan yaan." *Very-bad-against-law-person.*

"Ndioh gwok haat yee," spat Lao. *Foreign beggar.*

Kao Kan grasped Indy around the neck, but Jones cold-cocked him with a left hook. One of Lao's henchmen pulled Indy up from behind and, in so doing, kicked the vital blue liquid across the floor. Kao Kan's gun fell under the table.

A number of issues were racing through Willie's mind at this point: Lao was a scum she was glad to be rid of; she could forget about keeping her job at this place; she'd been right about this Jones character from the beginning; and if she kept a cool head, she might just get away with the diamond.

She stuck her hand into the fray on the table, picked up the diamond. She hardly had time to feel it, though, before Indy and the henchman he was wrestling crashed by her, knocking the jewel out of her hand, onto the dance floor.

"You fool," she gasped—talking simultaneously to Indy and herself—and dove after her fleeting fortune.

The band began to play, as if they thought the party was just getting rolling.

Indy rolled onto the next table with Lao's guard. The strongarm punched him in the jaw, stunning him; Indy swung back blindly, striking the cigarette girl, who'd fallen on top of them. The henchman threw Indy off the table, into a dinner trolley that started wheeling, from his momentum, toward the bandstand.

He careened through the bedlam like a flying apparition. The wind against his face revived him some, cooled the toxic perspiration on his forehead. The people he passed were starting to look a little distorted to him, though. He saw the vial on the floor— or did he imagine it?—but sailed right on by.

His flight was halted abruptly by crashing into the bandstand. He got up in time to see Lao's guard about to nab him, so he grabbed the big double bass in time to bash the guard into oblivion.

He stood there a moment, getting his bearings, when his eyes fell upon the vial, lying out there in the midst of the melee. He jumped for it.

In that moment, it was kicked away. In the next moment, Indy came up on his hands and knees facing Willie on *her* hands and knees.

"The antidote," said Indy.

"The diamond," Willie responded.

Indy noticed the stone near his hand, but it was immediately kicked between a dozen pairs of legs.

"Nuts," muttered Willie, crawling off after it. Indy plowed on in the opposite direction.

Lao finally made it past the shouting throng to the front door, and shouted. Almost instantly a cadre of his hoodlums ran in, awaiting instruction.

The band played on (minus the bass). Right on cue, the twelve dancing girls shuffled gaily out of the dragon's mouth and down onto the dance floor. Some party.

Indy chose the same cue to push himself up off the floor, and into the chorus line. He was feeling quite faint now. The sight of Lao's men pouring through the entrance carrying hatchets gave him a new surge of adrenaline, however; he was able to stumble back over to the bandstand.

Three hatchet men hurled their weapons at him, but he ducked behind one of the statues. Quickly, he grabbed a cymbal and sailed it back at a fourth hatchet-bearer, hitting the assassin in the head, knocking him cold. Knocking him very cold, in fact; the thug slumped into a huge ice bucket, scattering ice cubes all over the floor.

All over the diamond. Willie moaned with frustration, scrabbling through hundreds of ice nuggets, searching desperately for the now camouflaged diamond. What she found was the blue vial.

From the stage, Indy saw her pick it up. "Stay there!" he yelled at her. Please.

Their eyes met. It was a moment of decision for Willie. Who was this guy? He'd come into her life ten minutes ago, come on to her, held a fork on her, given her a touch of her first major-league precious stone, cost her her man (no loss) and her job (no sweat), and now she held his life in her hand. And he did have those eyes.

She stuck the vial down the front of her dress for safekeeping.

But no way was she going to stop looking for that diamond. She trudged off once more through the piles of ice.

Kao Kan woke up. He found his gun on the floor, turned slowly, saw Indy. Still a bit unsteady, he raised the gun, to fire across the room.

Indy saw him in time, though. He backed up to the side of the stage, pulled the release rope hanging there. And then, madly, with dream-slowness and a sense of disjointed dream-logic, balloons began floating down from the ceiling. Hundreds of colored balloons. Kao Kan lost sight of his target behind the curtain of this stately barrage.

They obscured everything in their steady, deliberate drift. Indy moved laterally, toward the place Willie had recently occupied. No Willie there, though. Only two more thugs.

One karate-chopped him, but he put the goon down with a jab to the solar plexus. He threw the other one into an angry waiter, and slumped against the balcony wall.

The poison was eating him up. He felt ashen pale, trembly. His stomach was cramping and he wanted to pass out. No, no. He had to find Willie. He had to get the vial.

He threw a glass of cold water on his face. It helped a little.

This was beginning to turn into a real situation, now. He saw four more gang members run in.

Kao Kan, meanwhile, was in a fury. He wanted his brother's murderer dead, but his arm was still shaking too much to get off a clear shot. Fortunately, he noticed that one of his gang cohorts was carrying a machine gun. Maniacally he raced over to the stairs, took the weapon from the man, and walked into the confusion, shouting, "Where is he? I'll kill him."

People who saw the gun started to scatter. The balloons were thinning out, now, too; in a few moments, Kao Kan and Indy saw each other. As Kao began to shoot, Indy dove over the ledge of the balcony, near the huge hanging gong.

Bullets tore into the balcony. Indy huddled behind the great bronze shield. People were screaming, hitting the floor, heading for cover.

When the first burst was over, Indy leaped over to the statue of the lounging warrior, pulled the golden broadsword from its hand, and with two quick slashes cut the cords that suspended the giant gong from the ceiling; it dropped to the floor with a resounding CHUNG.

He jumped down behind it as bullets entered its bronze face. Then, sheltering himself on its back side, he slowly wheeled it across the floor, toward where Willie was still scurrying furiously.

Machine-gun bullets kept clanging against the surface of Indy's enormous shield. As it rolled, it gained momentum; he had to run to stay hidden. It made a monster noise, this lumbering gong, deflecting the gunfire.

Willie heard the awesome sound and looked up

to see the mammoth disk bearing down on her. *So this is it*, she thought. *Crushed by a renegade gong during a cabaret riot.*

Indy grabbed her arm at the last second, though, pulling her behind the shield with him. Bullets ricocheted as Lao's men jockeyed for better firing positions among the overturned tables.

Willie hollered. Indy looked ahead. Directly before them stood an entire panel of floor-to-ceiling stained-glass windows. She shouted, "I don't want—"

But there was no time to debate. The rolling gong crashed through the towering panes; a moment later, Indy grabbed Willie around the waist and dove with her through the opening.

It was free-fall for ten feet, followed by a tumble down a sloping tiled roof; and then over the edge.

Their entwined bodies plummeted two more stories, ripping through a second-floor awning, smashing through a bamboo balcony, finally thudding to rest into the backseat of a convertible Duesenberg parked directly in front of the building.

Willie sat up in a hurry, completely amazed to be alive, to find herself staring into the equally astonished face of a twelve-year-old Chinese boy wearing a New York Yankees baseball cap, staring back at her from the front seat.

"Wow! Holy smoke! Crash landing!" said Short Round.

"Step on it, Short Round!" said Indy, rising more slowly.

"Okey doke, Indy," said the kid. "Hold on to your potatoes!"

With a great grin, Short Round swiveled around,

turned his baseball cap bill-backwards, and stepped on the gas.

Tires squealing, they tore off into the Shanghai night.

2

A Boy's Life

Short Round was just having an average day.

He'd gotten up early that morning—around noon—and gone to work. Work was on the premises of the Liu Street opium den.

Short Round didn't really have all that much to do there in the afternoons. Only a few customers at such a daylight hour, plus a few more sleeping it off from the night before. Short Round brought them tea; or walked them out to rickshaws; or guarded their clothing in the next room, for pennies—except that occasionally he helped himself to more than pennies from the goods he was guarding: occasionally he helped himself to articles of interest.

Among other things, Short Round was a thief.

Not a thief in the strictest sense, of course. He liked to think of himself more along the lines of Robin Hood, the hero in the movie he'd seen seven or eight times at the Tai-Phung Theater. It was simply that one of the poor people he gave to was himself.

At least, such was his thought that morning, during the Liu Street den's long afternoon lull. The sweet smoke hung in thin layers above two stupefied patrons who slumped on the bare wooden cots, one an old Chinese man, one a young Belgian. Short Round was sitting on their belongings in the adjoining room, wondering about breakfast, when it occurred to him there might be something to eat in the Belgian man's bag. He was just rifling through it when the bag's owner walked in. The man did not seem pleased.

Nor did he seem dopey. In fact, he seemed rather irate. Short Round knew enough about these encounters to know that explanations were not usually fruitful, so he left by the window . . . with the Belgian's passport stuck (quite by accident) to his fingers.

The Belgian chased after him.

Short Round loved a good chase. Made him feel wanted. He ran down the rear alley, the indignant client on his tail. Over a fence, up two more winding back streets; the man stayed with him. Up a fire escape along the side of an ancient wood building—all the way up, to the roof. The Belgian was right behind.

Short Round took off across the roofs. Sloping, tiled, gabled—this was the most fun yet; he slid, scooted, swung around chimneys like a monkey in the trees. Rooftops were Short Round's specialty.

His pursuer lost distance, but not sight. Short Round came to the edge of the last roof: sheer drop, four stories. The Belgian closed the gap. Short Round scurried up the slope, over the peak, down the other side. Same drop-off.

Except a few feet below, coming out the top window of the building, was a clothesline, stringing across the alley to the window of the building on the other side.

Just like Robin Hood! Wow! Holy smoke! Short Round hopped down to the clothesline, dangled there a second, then brachiated along a string of flapping silk pajamas to the window across the way while his pursuer swore in Flemish from the roof ledge behind him.

Short Round dove in the window, turned, gave the fuming man a million-dollar smile in payment for his passport, and called out to him: "Very funny! Very funny big joke!"

The man was not amused. People had no sense of humor anymore. Short Round apologized for the disturbance to the incredulous family he'd just barged in on. Then with propriety that seemed incongruous, considering his flying entrance, he bowed, and left by the front door.

Out on the street, shadows were growing long. Fish vendors were packing up, their wares beginning to smell; night people hadn't yet begun to stir. This was Short Round's favorite time. It was the hour of the doves.

Every day around now, hundreds of doves would accumulate in the courtyard of the monastery near the Gung Ho Bar. They made the most wondrous aggregate cooing, like the murmurings of a thousand satisfied Persian cats. It was a sound Short Round associated with being rocked by his mother, though he couldn't remember why. He hadn't had any family for many years.

Except Dr. Jones, of course. Dr. Jones was his family now.

Short Round suspected Indy was actually a reincarnation of the lower god Chao-pao, He-Who-Discovers-Treasures. But Short Round himself claimed Chao-pao as an ancestor, so he and Indy were closely related in any case.

He walked out of the Place of Doves, over to the Gung Ho Bar. This was where he and Indy had first met. He entered the bar. In the back booth, sipping a cup of ginseng tea, Indy was now seated, waiting. Short Round ran up to him with a big grin, took the seat opposite.

"Indy, I get passport for Wu Han!" he whispered excitedly. He handed over the Belgian's passport.

Indy looked it over, raised his eyebrows. "Shorty, where'd you get this? I thought I told you not to steal anymore."

"No steal," the boy protested. "Man give me. He not need anymore."

Short Round looked so ingenuous, so hurt, Indy almost believed him. In any case, he pocketed the documents for Wu Han.

Short Round beamed. That was one of the reasons he loved Indy. He and Indy, they were birds of a feather: they both had a knack for transferring the ownership of lost items, finding new homes for valuables that had resided in one place too long.

Indy was going to find a new home for Short Round, for example. He was going to take Short Round to America.

Indy squinted at him now. "Okay, kid, you sure I can count on you for the plane tickets?" He gave the boy money to purchase their tickets.

"Easy like pie, Indy. I just get my Uncle Wong's

car; then I talk to ticket man; then I wait for you at club."

"Right out front." Indy nodded. "An hour before dawn. You got a watch?"

"Sure okay."

"Well, you make sure to tell your uncle thanks for the use of his car again."

"Oh, he don't mind. We leave for America soon?"

"Yeah, pretty soon. Delhi, first. Now get going; I've got to meet a man about a box."

Short Round left the bar; Indy stayed. Short Round ran six blocks to the house of a German diplomat he knew superficially—knew not at all, actually, except he'd shined the man's shoes at one of the classier brothels the week before, and there had overheard the honorable consul tell the madame that he was leaving town for a fortnight to visit relatives in Alsace.

When Short Round got to the house, he walked around back. He crawled into the garage through the small cat-door that was cut in the bottom panel of the side entrance. Inside the garage, he spent about ten minutes playing with the young cat, dragging a little woolen mouse on a string back and forth in front of it, until it pounced. When the excited kitten finally retreated, with its prize, to a hidden corner under the stairs, Short Round opened the garage doors wide. Then he hot-wired the car.

It was a cream-colored 1934 Duesenberg Auburn convertible, an easy ride to wire. Easy or not, he'd already taken this one for a spin with Indy several times this week. Now he hunkered down under the dash, crossing leads until the connection sparked and the engine roared into life. It made Short Round feel like the boy in the fairy tale who lived in the belly of a dragon: he closed his eyes, listened to the pistons rumbling, smelled the smoke of the electrical short-circuit, felt the dark enclosure wrap over him in the shape of a fire-hardened dragon-stomach....

Scaring himself, he squirmed up to the seat, put the car in reverse, backed out of the garage, let the car idle, closed the garage doors again, turned down the circular drive, and headed for the open road.

He could barely see above the steering wheel or reach the pedals, but barely was all he needed. The city streets became residential, then quickly rural, in the fading afternoon light. This was Short Round's second favorite time of day: when the sun burned orange as a red coal, just before the earth gobbled it up again for the night.

By early evening he was standing in a small British airport office, negotiating for three tickets with a small British airport official named Weber.

"I hardly think I could make room for someone of *your* stature," the officious Briton began.

Short Round gave him most of Indiana's money. "Not for me. For Dr. Jones, the famous professor. This very important government case. I his assistant."

Weber still looked skeptical, but took the money. "Well, I'll see what I can do."

"You do good, Dr. Jones put you in his book. Maybe you get a medal." He winked.

Weber seemed taken aback by this strange little manipulator. "I'll do what I can, but I'm not certain I can get three seats on the same plane with such short notice."

Short Round winked again, and slipped Weber the last of Indy's wad of bills as a bribe. He also let

Weber see the dagger half-hidden in his belt. Weber felt distinctly disconcerted accepting a payoff from a twelve-year-old gangster; nonetheless, he took the money.

"Yes, I'm sure the accommodations can be arranged." He smiled. He wondered when the London Office was going to transfer him back to civilization.

Short Round bowed to Weber most graciously, then shook the man's hand, then saluted smartly, his fingertips to the visor of his baseball cap. Then he ran back to the Duesenberg and drove back to town.

He left the car parked in the warehouse of a friend who owed him a favor. Night was just opening its eyes. Short Round thought of the daytime as a sleeping rascal who awoke, each night, with a great hunger. Short Round's third favorite time was all night.

He ambled down to the docks. A boy had to be careful here—boys were much in demand, for forced sea duty, or other disreputable occupations—but it was a good place for a wily boy to get a free supper. And, like the night, Short Round was getting hungry.

He scavenged a small, flat plank from the garbage behind one of the bars, and took it down to where the oily water lapped right up against the quais. He squatted there in the shadows, his feet submerged, waiting. After five minutes passed quietly—during which time he prayed to Naga, the Dragon-King, who inhabited and guarded this sea—he suddenly slapped the board against the surface of the water, hard, several times.

In a second, a juicy moonfish rose, belly-up, to the shallow, stunned by Short Round's concussions.

He grabbed the fish by the tail, yanked it out of the water, smacked it against the piling. Then, crouching in the sand a few feet away, he slit it open with his dagger, and feasted on the tender yellow meat. He wondered if they had moonfish in America.

Thinking of America made him think of movies. It was hours before he had to meet Indy yet, so he decided to wander down to the Tai-Phung Theater, to see if anything new was playing. The Tai-Phung showed mostly American films, mostly for the international crowd that populated the banking or diplomatic sections of the city. The Tai-Phung is where Short Round learned most of his English.

He couldn't read the marquee when he got there— he couldn't read at all, hardly, except for the little bits Indy was teaching him—but the letters looked different from the markings that had been there last time he'd looked, so he decided to go check it out.

He crawled in the high bathroom window at the back of the building by standing on two garbage cans outside. Once in, he lowered himself down to the toilet tank, then to the floor. He offered to shine the shoes of the man sitting, a bit shocked, on the pot, but the man politely refused. Short Round scooted under the door of the stall, and out into the theater.

He sat in an aisle seat, near the exit, for quick departure if that should be necessary. He slumped down so the ushers who knew him by face wouldn't spot him right away. He popped a lump of bubble gum in his mouth. He settled back to watch the movie.

It was a nifty show. This private eye named Nick kept making very funny big jokes to his wife, Nora, very pretty lady. They had a silly dog, too, named

Asta. Nick was drinking another martini at a big party where the bad guys were lurking, when a fancy couple sat down right in front of Short Round, blocking his view.

He was about to move to another seat when he noticed the woman put her purse down in the space between the two chairs. This looked too easy to pass up. Short Round waited ten minutes—until they got absorbed in the film—then reached forward and slid the pocketbook back to his lap.

It was a silver lamé evening bag with a mother-of-pearl clasp. Short Round clicked it open, quickly rummaged through it. Wow! What great luck! There was a jeweled makeup compact with a small watch set into its back. Just what he needed to check the time for his meeting with Indy—when the little hand was on the four, and the big hand on the twelve. (Indy was teaching him numbers, too. Numbers were easier.)

This was a very good omen: it portended well for the rest of the night. Short Round gave a brief prayer of thanks to Chao-pao, his patron deity, He-Who-Discovers-Treasures. Then he stood, began panting loudly, and fell in the aisle, draping his arm over the woman's chair.

"My word!" she gasped.

"Lady, big man just steal your purse!" Short Round panted, dropping the purse at her feet. "I catch him and take back for you. He hit me, but I get away. Here your purse." He nudged it toward her with his knee, then he collapsed.

"You poor child!" she said, quickly looking in the wallet at the bottom of the handbag. All the money was still there.

"Shhh!" said her companion, trying to ignore the

distraction, feeling it was always the wisest course to disregard the overtures of these street urchins.

The woman arched an eyebrow at her escort. Short Round whimpered in apparent pain. The woman gave Short Round two dollars. "There you are, you sweet thing," she spoke as if she were confiding. "That's for being so brave and honest."

"Thanks, lady," said Short Round. He stuffed the bills in his pants, jumped up, ran out the door. The lady, briefly startled, went back to her movie.

Outside, the night was flexing. Paper lanterns, incense, jugglers, hookers, hawkers. Short Round, feeling a lot like Nick Charles, approached a stree-twalker who had one slit up the side of her dress, another up the side of her smile.

"Hey, sugar, got a cigarette?" He winked at her.

She was about to retort, had a second thought, reached into her bag, pulled out a stick of gum, and flipped it to him.

"Oh, boy!" he exclaimed, pocketing the prize. "Thanks, lady!" He ran off, ready for anything. What a night!

For a dollar he bought a top that played music and flashed lights as it spun. Three boys went after him for it, though. He had to hit one of them over the head with the toy as he was climbing over a fence to get away. End of chase; end of toy.

He was left holding the broken top handle. This he threw as far as he could, back down the alley he'd been chased, and that was pretty far. Someday he'd be as good a pitcher as the great Lefty Grove: Short Round, too, was a southpaw.

His other dollar he gave to an old woman who sat, begging, on a doorstep. It upset him to see old beggars, especially grandmothers. Family was more important than anything, of course. His own grand-mother was gone, but what if *she* were begging on a stoop somewhere. It was important to remember this.

The old woman bowed to Short Round; he thanked her for allowing him to honor her.

It began to rain, a fine rain. Short Round hurried back to the warehouse in which he'd parked the Duesenberg. Several men sat in a circle near the far wall. One of them was casting the I Ching.

Short Round watched him for an hour. The man threw the yarrow stalks for each person there, but when Short Round asked for his own path to be read, the man refused.

Short Round took a nap behind some bales of tea for a while, put to sleep by the cheery mumblings of a band of sailors throwing dice in a nearby alcove. Dice, I Ching: same thing. When he awoke, he saw a young couple kissing beside another stack of bales against the wall. He watched them for a few min-utes. They seemed very happy. He wondered if they had any children.

From the doorway, Short Round heard the static of an old radio. He walked over. The small box sat on the ground plugged into the wall; beside it a drunk American sailor crouched, tuning it to an almost inaudible station that replayed smuggled American recordings. Breaking up over the air waves now was another adventure of The Shadow, who knew what evil lurked in the hearts of men, and who could cloud men's minds. Shorty loved this program; he listened whenever he could. The sailor kicked him away, though. This was apparently a private show.

Anyway, it seemed like it was getting late. He looked at the watch he'd found: time to go. He started up the car and eased it out into traffic. The rain had stopped.

He got to the club right when he was supposed to. No Indy, though. The doorman tried to make him move the car away from the front door, but he gave the doorman the jeweled compact-timepiece, so the doorman said he could stay there for a bit, if he didn't cause any trouble.

Then Indy dropped in. With the lady.

"Wow! Holy smoke! Crash landing!" said Short Round.

"Step on it, Short Round!" said Indy.

Tires squealing, they tore off into the Shanghai night.

Willie couldn't believe it. "For crying out loud, a *kid's* driving the car?!"

"Relax, I've been giving him lessons," Indy said nonchalantly.

"Oh, that makes me feel a *lot* safer," she nodded.

As Short Round swerved around the next corner, Willie was thrown against Indiana. Without losing a beat, he put his hand down the front of her dress.

Willie became indignant. "Listen, we just met, for crissake." Some men...

"Don't get your hopes up. Where's the antidote?" It was hard feeling around in there; his fingertips were numb with poison. Too bad.

He rubbed the glass vial with his palm, rolled it into his fingers, pulled it from her bra, screwed off the lid, tipped it to his lips, and swallowed. "Ech."

"You don't look very good."

"Poison never agrees with me." He wiped his mouth on his sleeve. "Short Round, pull a right and head for the Wang Poo bridge."

"Check! Gotcha!" the kid shouted back. When

he drove fast, he tried to look just like James Cagney.

Indy peered out the back window and noticed a large black sedan in pursuit. "Looks like we got company."

Willie was suddenly depressed. If Lao caught her now, he'd *really* be hacked off. The club was a shambles, she'd lost the diamond, the kid was going to crash the car any minute, she had two broken nails...that was it. The last straw. She could cope with all the rest, but how was a girl supposed to get a job singing when she looked like—

She looked at herself in the reflection of the side window. Even worse than she thought. Tears began to well up in her eyes; tears of anger. "Look at what you've done to me," she seethed. "My lipstick is smeared, I broke two nails, there's a run in my stocking."

Gunfire shattered the rear window, spraying them with glass. Indy and Willie crouched low; Short Round was already too low in his seat to be visible from behind.

"Somehow I think you've got bigger problems," muttered Indiana, reaching for his shoulder bag. He pulled out a pistol, began firing back through the broken window. "There, Shorty!" he barked. "Through the tunnel!"

They screeched through the darkened tunnel. The pursuit car stayed right with them, its headlights burning like spectral eyes.

"What're we going to do?" cried Willie. "Where're we going!" The magnitude of the calamity was just setting in.

"The airport," Indy snapped. "No, look out, Short Round! Left, *left*!" He reached over the front seat, put a hand on the wheel, helped Short Round navigate. Then, more softly: "You're doin' all right, kid."

Willie sank lower.

The Duesenberg emerged on a crowded square: ten thousand merchants, beggars, hookers, sailors, thieves, buyers, and coolies with rickshaws wandered gaily amidst the jumble of bright paper lanterns, calligraphed banners, storefronts, and produce stands. They all scattered when the Duesenberg came roaring by.

Some of them scattered back over the street in the Duesenberg's wake—enough to totally clog the thoroughfare by the time the black sedan came barreling in. It crashed headlong into a vegetable stand, then swerved and skidded against the curb, finally coming to a halt in a swarm of peddlers.

Indy peered out the back window. "Looks like chop suey back there." Willie was afraid to look.

They put some distance on the stalled pursuer. Out onto the highway now; some fast, open countryside.

"Shorty, you called the airport?"

"Sure, Indy. Mr. Weber get seats for you, me, and Wu Han."

"Wu Han's not coming, Shorty."

Short Round considered this. Wu Han wouldn't have run; he was too loyal. Therefore he was either dead, captured, or holding off the bad guys—all very honorable occupations for Wu Han to have chosen. In any case, it was up to Short Round alone now to protect their beloved comrade and spirit-brother. "Don't worry, Indy," he assured. "Short Round number-one bodyguard now."

Willie braved a glance out the back. Far in the distance, tiny headlights rounded a curve and followed them. "I'll take the extra seat," she said dryly. Her options seemed distinctly limited. "Where are we going, anyway?"

"Siam," said Indy, reloading his gun.

"Siam?" she complained. "I'm not dressed for Siam." She wanted to complain more, actually, but no gods, demigods, or justices in the whole pagan universe seemed to want to listen or care just now, much less the deranged yahoo beside her. She looked over at him suspiciously. Outside, on the road, a sign flew by: NANG TAO AIRPORT. The headlights behind them seemed to be gaining.

Well, maybe it would work out. She'd never been to Siam. . . .

Short Round wheeled the car up a gravel drive toward the airfield. Just past a small cargo area. Out on the runway, a trimotor was revving its engines. The Duesenberg squealed to a stop on the apron; the three of them jumped out. Short Round carried Indy's shoulder bag.

At the boarding gate, the young English airline official ran up to meet them. "Dr. Jones, I'm Weber, I spoke with your . . . assistant." He eyed Short Round curiously for a moment, then continued. "I managed to find three seats; Unfortunately they're in a cargo plane full of poultry."

"Is he kidding?" Willie protested.

"Madam," Weber began officiously, "it was the best I could do on such short—" He stopped suddenly, and smiled. "My heavens, aren't you Willie Scott, the famous vocalist?"

Willie was completely taken aback, then instantly

charmed: here, smack-dab in the middle of the worst day in a while, was a fan. "Well, yes, I am, actually." She blushed.

"Miss Scott," Weber fawned, "I've so enjoyed your performances. In fact, if you don't mind my saying it—"

Willie was just beginning to think it maybe hadn't been quite such a bad day after all when Jones shot off his mouth again.

"You can sign autographs, doll. Shorty and I have to go."

Indy and Shorty took off for the plane. Willie hesitated for a second, but quickly found her allegiance when she saw the black sedan squeal into the airport. In her sweetest voice, with a look of majesty worn well, she said to Weber, "It's always swell meeting a fan, Mr. Weber, but I really must run now." And then, coarsely, to Indy: "Goddammit, wait for me!"

She hightailed it toward the plane. Weber waved. Willie jumped on.

The black sedan screeched to a halt at the fence of the loading area. Lao Che hopped out, followed by several henchmen with guns. The commotion— and the guns—aroused the notice of two airport policemen, who slowly wandered toward the car. Lao Che looked across the tarmac at the taxiing plane in time to see Indy give him a neat salute and slam the cargo bay shut.

Lao Che's men looked to him for orders, for rage. He only smiled, though. As the plane swung around to gain speed up the runway, he could plainly see its legend inscribed along the fuselage of the blind side: LAO CHE AIR FREIGHT.

Rolling past, the pilot saw Lao standing on the

field, and saluted his boss. Laughing deeply, Lao Che returned the salute.

The plane lifted off with a roar, silhouetted crisply against the first orange light of dawn.

They flew west.

Willie huddled in her damp, sequinned dress, looking for warmth while dozens of crated and nervous chickens kept attacking her. "Quit pecking at me, you dumb clucks, or you're gonna be sitting on plates with mashed potatoes." This was really too much.

The worst part was it brought her back to her beginnings—on a chicken farm in Missouri. Dirty, no-account, nowhere chickens.

Her mother used to tell her that was where she belonged, that no amount of dreaming, or aching to be somewhere else, was ever going to get her off the farm. It would take a miracle to do that, her mother told her, and there were no such things as miracles.

It was no miracle that Willie won the county beauty queen contest when she was eighteen, though: she was just simply the most beautiful girl in the county.

With her prize money she went to New York, to be an actress and a dancer. No miracles there, though; everyone in New York wanted that, it seemed. So Willie drifted west.

She fell in with bad company in Chicago, had to leave in sort of a hurry. Which got her off on the wrong foot in Hollywood—which is a bad foot to start off on if you're a dancer.

So it was either back to Missouri or keep drifting west. And one thing Willie knew for certain was that of all the places in the world where miracles didn't exist, they didn't exist in Missouri.

She hitched a ride with a snazzy dresser who promised her the Orient was wide open. Well, that much was true, she'd found out: like a big hole.

She never saw a miracle in Shanghai, either, but things had finally begun working out. She'd developed a nice little local reputation; she had a following. She had a suitor or two. She had prospects.

But that was all ancient history. Now, instead of prospects, she had retrospects. Now she had chicken feathers in her mouth. And it tasted just like Missouri.

The door opened at the rear of the plane; out stepped Indiana Jones. He had changed.

Now he wore a beat-up leather jacket over a khaki shirt, work-pants and work-boots, a gray snap-brim hat, a leather bag across his shoulder, an old army holster at his waist. He walked forward carrying the rolled-up tuxedo in one hand, and a coiled bullwhip in the other.

He sat down between Willie and Shorty, dumping the formal wear on the floor, hanging the whip up on a coat peg.

"So, what're you supposed to be, a lion tamer?" sneered Willie with some amusement. Men were such boys.

"Since I was nice enough to let you tag along, why don't you give your mouth a rest. Okay, doll?" He patted her leg condescendingly. She was definitely starting to get on his nerves.

She removed his hand from her thigh. This guy obviously had only one thing on his mind—and this wasn't the time, it wasn't the place, it wasn't the guy. She picked up his dinner jacket from the floor. "I'm freezing. What do you mean, tag along? From the minute you walked into the nightclub, you haven't been able to keep your eyes off me." She started toward the rear of the plane, wrapping the coat around her shoulders.

"Oh, yeah?" said Indy.

He smiled, lay back against a wall of chicken crates, tipped his hat down over his eyes, and went to sleep.

The cockpit door opened a crack. The copilot stared intently into the cargo hold.

He saw Willie sleeping on a pillow of sequins near the rear, curled up now in Indy's dark formal pants, white dress shirt, and tuxedo jacket; Indy was asleep portside, his hat over his face, chicken feathers dotting his coat, and Shorty was sleeping peacefully beside him in sneakers, baseball cap, quilted pants, and a frayed, cotton coolie jacket, his head resting on Indy's shoulder.

The copilot looked over at the pilot, who was receiving radio instructions from his employer. The pilot looked back at the copilot and nodded.

The copilot picked up a large wrench, hefting it as he scrutinized Jones. After a moment, his second thoughts got the better of him; he put down the wrench and drew a knife from his belt.

As the copilot started out the door, Indiana rolled over. The copilot pulled back.

The pilot swore in Chinese, handed his assistant a .45 automatic. The copilot studied the gun, asked if the woman and the kid had to go too. The pilot nodded. The copilot felt this would engender some

39

bad karma, and said so. The pilot vehemently disagreed. They had words. References were made to each other's ancestors.

Ultimately the pilot took his gun back, ordered the copilot to take over the controls, and went to do the job himself.

Indiana still slept soundly. As the pilot took a step toward him, an egg rolled out of a high overhead crate and fell—fell two inches to a wad of rag, then rolled end over end along an inclined plank, dropped to a finely balanced nest, teeter-tottered down to a narrow ledge, hovered an instant, and finally plunged. Without waking, without moving a muscle more than necessary, Indy held out his hand and caught the egg before it hit the ground.

Indiana Jones was not without flaw, but he had a sense for falling eggs.

It was a feat that stopped the pilot in his tracks. Amazed and afraid of this dangerous sorcerer, he backed up two steps, smiling sheepishly at the copilot. They discussed the matter calmly; they made suggestions. They had their orders. But they decided it was a matter best left to the gods.

The pilot pushed the lever on the instrument panel that emptied the fuel tanks. The copilot fitted them both up with parachutes. Then, quietly, they walked to the rear of the plane.

Willie awoke in time to blearily see the copilot enter the aft bay, closing the curtains behind him. She rolled over to go back to sleep, when she noticed the pilot emerge from the cockpit, walk back, and disappear through the same curtains.

It seemed rather odd to her. It wasn't that big an airplane; she didn't think any more crew could fit up there. Hmm. No more crew. "I wonder who's flying the plane, then."

She got up, walked forward, stuck her head inside the cockpit door. Nobody flying the plane.

She slammed the door shut with a yelp. "There's nobody flying the plane!"

Short Round, ever vigilant, woke up as soon as she shouted. Indy, still groggy from the aftereffects of the poison, kept sleeping.

Willie rushed to the back of the plane. She parted the curtains. There stood the two and only crew on the brink of the open cargo door, parachutes strapped to their backs.

"Oh, my God! Don't go! Help, Indiana! Wake up, the pilot's bailing out!"

Shorty ran over to her. Wow! No joke! The pilot was abandoning ship.

Groggily, Indy opened his eyes. "We there already?"

In a flash Willie was shaking him, waking him, beseeching him. "Nobody driving . . . jumping . . . parachutes. . . . Do something!" This cowboy had to be good for something; surely this was a flight jacket he was wearing. Surely he knew how to fly this old bus.

Indiana got up and ran back to the open curtains. Nobody there. Just two chutes billowing open in the clear sky beyond.

He ran up to the cockpit, Willie at his heels. In an instant he appraised the situation and slipped into the pilot's seat, at the controls, with absolute confidence.

Willie was teary-eyed with gratitude. Laughing, nodding, seeing there was a reason, after all for this dubious doctor to exist. With a sigh of relief to her own question, she asked: "You know how to fly?"

Indy surveyed the control panel, turned a couple of knobs, flipped a switch, took the wheel. "No." Then, ingenuously: "Do you?"

Willie turned white; she felt her stomach rising.

Indy flashed a big bad smile, though. "Just kidding, sweetheart. I got everything under control. Altimeter: check. Stabilizer: roger. Air speed: okay. Fuel—"

There was a long pause. Willie hadn't exactly gotten over his little joke about not knowing how to fly yet, so she was in no mood for humor now. But then this silence on Indy's part did not, in any case, sound like a humorous silence.

"Fuel?" said Willie. "Fuel? What about the fuel?"

Indiana stood up slowly. Willie followed his gaze out the window: the last engine sputtered to a stop. All the props were motionless. The plane began to nose downward.

"We've got a problem," said Indiana.

He walked past Willie, into the hold. "Shorty!"

Short Round ran up breathless. "I already check, Indy. No more parachutes." Maybe they could grow wings, like when the Monkey-God Wo-Mai gave wings to the silkworms so they could become moths, to escape their earthly prison.

Indy began to rummage through all the storage lockers.

In the cockpit, Willie was jerked rudely out of her catatonia by the almighty ludicrous vision of a snowy mountain looming immediately ahead of the windshield. "Indiana!" she bellowed, less as a call for help than as a last moment of human contact before annihilation.

The gods were generous, though. The plane barely missed the peak, knocking a noseful of snow from the highest pinnacle, clearing the crest by inches.

Willie's heart nearly stopped. She ran from the cockpit, to see Indy pulling a huge wad of yellow canvas from one of the storage bins. Printed across its side were the words EMERGENCY LIFE RAFT. "Are you nuts?" she screamed at him in fury.

He ignored her. "Give me a hand, Shorty," he told the boy.

The two of them dragged the folded canvas over to the open cargo door, as Willie kept shouting, "Are you crazy, a life raft! We're not *sinking*, we're crashing!"

"Get over here, damn it!" he ordered. "Short Round, come on, grab onto me tight."

Short Round encircled Indy's waist from behind. This crash would be better than anything in *Wings*, which Shorty had seen four times.

Willie hesitated a moment before deciding that no matter what else, she didn't want to die alone.

"Wait for me!" the little girl in her called. She grabbed her gold dress—no point in not having something to wear, just in case—ran over and threw her arms around Indiana's neck, so that she and Shorty were both hugging him from behind.

Indy clutched the bunched-up life raft in front of him as he perused the mountainside rushing close, now, beneath their sinking aircraft. Fifteen feet above the ground. Ten, and diving. Seven.

Indy jumped with all his strength, pulling the inflation cord.

Short Round closed his eyes, ready to fly.

3

The Sacred Stone

They spilled from the hatch. As the plane skimmed over the slopes out of control, the raft popped open into its full, bloated form, acting suddenly as a spoiler—a great bulbous kite, soaring against the rushing air, dangling these three terrified souls over eternity.

Short Round made a secret promise to Madame Wind, Feng-p'o, the Celestial Being responsible for keeping them aloft with her bags of swirling breezes.

A hundred yards away, the cargo plane kissed the earth, exploding into a tremendous conflagration of rock, steel, roast chicken. A moment later, the life raft skidded into a snowbank, bounced, flew, hit again, and took off at speed down the pristine slopes.

Indiana held on to the front while Willie and Shorty each had handfuls of ripcords. They rocketed down the mountainside like a bobsled for a few minutes, finally crossing the timberline. It was snowy forest, now. Willie looked up for less than a second before deciding she didn't want to look again.

Shorty was scared and excited all at once. This was just like the foiled escape in *Ice Creatures From Venus*. But Indy would pull them through. Short Round didn't have to look to know that. Indy was the ultimate clutch hitter—probably better, even, than Lou Gehrig.

They bounced over a snow-hidden log and took to the air again, directly toward a large tree. Indy tugged fiercely at the perimeter rope, rolled on his side, somehow managed to swerve the raft so it caromed off the snow-drifted edge of the tree. They slid straight down the next bank.

The downhill run continued. They slowed considerably, splashing through first a small stream, then some leafy ground cover. When they entered a clearing at half-speed, finally near the end of the ordeal, Indy chanced to smile at the others with relief.

"Indy, you the greatest," admired Short Round. Better even than Robin Hood.

Indy beamed at Willie. "Sometimes I amaze even myself."

"I'll bet," she replied weakly.

"Indy!" Short Round yelled.

Indy turned just as they crashed through a tangle of bushes, becoming airborne once again—over the edge of a sheer cliff. None of them looked down.

They dropped in a gentle parabolic curve for probably not as long as it felt, coming finally to rest, with a splash, on a wide bed of water. White water.

The raft plunged immediately into the raging torrent, battering rocks, spinning over roaring waves, twisting between narrow gaps of craggy stone. They held on tightly, choking and sputtering, as the rapids tore them down falls, into boulders, over thundering cascades.

Every ounce of energy was devoted to holding on. No thought to steering, to repositioning, to prayers or recriminations. Just keeping those fingers closed on those ropes.

And then there was one heart-stopping bounce—and the raft seemed to slow. It drifted out of the main stream, over toward a backwater, a sort of small bay on the river. The three bedraggled passengers lay totally still in the bottom of the raft.

Short Round, battered and exhausted, lifted his young head a few inches, to ascertain the safety of his charge. "Indy?"

Indiana coughed once. "Okay, Shorty. I'm okay."

Willie moaned. She was drenched to the bone—they all were—her hair soaked and stringy, her clothes dripping. She felt like a total mess.

"You all right?" Indiana asked her.

"No," she winced. "I'm not cut out for this kind of life." *It was nice of you to ask, though,* she thought. "Where are we, anyway?"

The raft floated to a gentle stop at the shore—more precisely, at a pair of dark legs standing on the shoreline.

Indy squinted up into the sun to see who was attached to the legs. "India," he whispered.

"Holy cow," Willie exclaimed. "India? How do you know we're in—" She rolled over to find herself staring up at the strange, withered face of an old, bony-thin man. She gasped.

The man wore a tattered robe. Around his neck

hung strings of fantastic beads. His skin was dark umber, aged as time. He looked like a witch doctor.

An eerie wind rose up howling all around them. Suddenly the old man placed his palms together—Willie jumped—and moved his wedded hands up to touch his forehead.

Willie and Short Round watched, mystified, as Indiana, in like manner, returned the shaman's silent greeting.

They walked now, the shaman and four turbaned peasants, followed by Indy, carrying his bullwhip; Short Round, carrying Indy's bag; and Willie, carrying her evening gown and heels. It was a gutted, rocky path they took, through barren, rolling hills. Scrub covered the landscape in patches; an occasional fruitless tree. The air smelled dusty.

Short Round walked comfortably, taking three paces to each of Indy's two. It wasn't easy following in the footsteps of such a one, but Short Round was up to the task, for he loved Indy. Indy had befriended him when he hadn't a friend, trusted him when he'd earned no trust. And Indy was going to take him to America.

They were on their way now. Short Round could hardly believe it. America: where everyone had shoes and hats, rode in cars, knew how to dance, shot straight, made jokes, played hard, held true, looked great, talked smart, ate well, took chances that paid off. That's where Short Round was going.

He'd guard Indy tenaciously until they got there. Then, once Indy didn't need a bodyguard anymore, Short Round figured he'd just be Indy's son; that way he could continue to take care of Indy without having to drive to work every day. The only problem with this plan was that if Indy became Shorty's father, a mother would be needed. A wife. Like yin needed yang. Like Nick Charles had Nora; Fred Astaire had Ginger Rogers. Robin and Marian. Gable and Harlow. Hsienpo and Ying-t'ai.

It was in the context of these envied and archetypal pairings that Short Round cast his eye on Willie in a new light.

She might be just right for Indy. She was pretty enough; she'd gone the distance, so far. She might do okay for a mom. She and Indy could adopt him, and they could all live on the Twentieth Century Limited, riding the rails back and forth to New York City. It could be a good life. Short Round would have to consider her carefully for the job. He would give it some thought.

Willie, meanwhile, was feeling enormous relief to be alive, even if it *was* in a big desolate nowhere. Several times during the past night she might as easily have been *dead* in a big desolate nowhere, and alive was definitely better. She felt the warm stone on her bare feet, she felt the glorious sun on her face, she felt absolutely in intimate touch with her very life. She felt hungry.

She wondered if Indy had any food in his bag or jacket. Walking faster, to catch up with him, she saw he was talking to the shaman.

Actually, the shaman was talking to Indy. "Mama okey enakan bala; gena hitiyey." Indiana wasn't exactly fluent in this dialect, but he understood it all right: "*I was waiting for you*," the shaman was saying. "*I saw it in a dream. I saw the aeroplane fall out of the sky by the river. I saw this in my dream.*" The old man kept repeating it over and over.

Willie reached them, listened a moment. "What'd he say?" she asked.

"They've been expecting me," said Indy. He looked puzzled.

"What do you mean—how?"

"The old man saw it in a dream."

"Dream," she scoffed. "Nightmare is more like it."

Indy squinted. "He said they were waiting at the river; they were waiting for the plane to fall down."

It was a bewildering statement. Willie shook her head. "Where was I? Was I in the dream?"

Indiana smiled at her. *Actresses*, he thought. He didn't know any more than she did, though, so there didn't seem much use in speculation. He just kept walking.

Willie, to ease her growing discomfort, just kept talking. "That's all? So how'd the dream end? How do we get out of here? When do we eat? I'm famished. What about me?"

The rocky ground turned to parched clay. Soon a hot wind swirled dust eddies all around them as the clay became thin soil, cracked and blighted. And finally, at the foot of these ravaged hills, they came to the village.

Mayapore village: like the soil, cracked and blighted.

They walked down a dessicated road through the town. A sense of devastation was palpable. Pitiful villagers stood in groups of three or four, watching the strangers being brought in. Watching without hope.

Women pulled buckets from dry wells, coming

up with sand. Miserable dogs skulked between huts of crumbling clay, daub, and wattle. Patient vultures lurked in a few scraggly trees. It was worse than a drought. It was a deathwatch.

Indiana noticed several villagers staring at Short Round, or pointing. A few haggard women seemed to be crying, though they shed no tears, for their bodies would not easily give up such precious water. Indy drew Shorty closer to him; these signs made him uneasy for the boy. Suddenly he realized why.

There were no children in the village.

Short Round saw it, too. He grew frightened by the odd attention, and worried for Indy's safety. He was Indy's bodyguard now, after all. He pulled closer, to keep an eye on his old friend, as the wretched population looked on.

They were shown into a small stone hut with three pallets on the floor. It had no windows, so was fractionally cooler than the arid exterior.

"Sleep now," the shaman told them, "for your journey has made you tired. Later will we eat, and talk. But for now, sleep." He left them without another word.

Indy translated for his companions.

"But I'm so hungry," whimpered Willie.

"Try counting lamb chops," suggested Indiana, lying down on the earth.

It must have worked, for soon they were all asleep.

Black clouds thick with ash clotted across the blood-red sunset.

Indiana, Willie, and Short Round sat tensely on broken stools in a hut with a thatched roof but no walls, only stone arches, encouraging whatever evening breeze there was to enter. Half a dozen elders were silhouetted on the dirt floor around them, some women, some men. Central to these was the village Chieftain, an ancient white-haired man who carried the anguish of all his people on his face.

The Chieftain gave commands. Three more women scuttled in, set wooden bowls before the visitors. No bowls were placed before the elders.

Willie looked expectant. "I sure hope this means dinner."

"Estuday. Estuday," Indy said to the women. *Thank you.*

As he spoke, the women were, in fact, ladling food into the dishes of the guests. It was a grayish gruel mixed with yellow rice and a bit of moldy fruit rind. Willie stared at it in despair. "I can't eat this."

"That's more food than these people have to eat in a week," Indy advised her. "They're starving."

"I can see that," she replied tersely. "What I fail to see is how my depriving them of this meal is going to help that plight—especially when it makes me gag just to look at it." As it was, the entire situation made her completely lose her appetite. How could she possibly take this meager portion from these wasting souls? It had never been this bad on the farm in Missouri; even so, these weathered faces brought back unwanted memories. Willie wished she were somewhere else.

"Eat it," Indy ordered.

"I'm not hungry," Willie insisted.

The village elders looked on.

Indy smiled thinly. "You're insulting them and embarrassing me. Eat it."

She could have cared less about embarrassing Jones, but she had no desire to add affront to the poverty of the village. She ate. They all did.

The Chieftain smiled with satisfaction. "Rest here before you go on," he said in English.

"We'd appreciate that," nodded Indiana. So the Chief spoke English. The British must have been nearby at one time.

"We not rest," Short Round piped up. "Indy is taking me to America. We go now. We go America." He just wanted to make sure that was the ground rule here, and understood as such, before anyone came up with any other thoughts on the matter.

"We go *to* America," Willie corrected his grammar. She hadn't actually let herself think of it before now, but it all of a sudden sounded like a pretty damn good idea. Manhattan, maybe.

"America. America," nodded the Chieftain, comprehending the notion only vaguely.

"Relax, kid," Indy said to Shorty, dropping his hat on the boy's head. Then to the chief: "Can you provide us with a guide to Delhi? I'm a professor and I have to get back to my university."

"Yes. Sajnu will guide you."

"Thank you."

The shaman spoke now. "On the way to Delhi you will stop at Pankot." It was spoken as if it were already fact, as if he were merely reporting something that had already happened.

Indiana noted the change in tenor. "Pankot isn't on the way to Delhi," he said carefully.

"There, you will go to Pankot Palace," the shaman went on as if Indy hadn't said a word.

Indy tried a new tack. "I thought the Palace had been deserted since 1857."

"No," the shaman corrected. "There is a new Maharajah now, and again the Palace has the dark light. It is as a hundred years ago. It is this place that kills my village."

Indy was having trouble picking up the thread. "I don't understand. What's happened here?"

The shaman spoke slowly, as if explaining to a small child. "The evil starts in Pankot. Then like monsoon it moves darkness over all country."

"The evil. What evil?" said Indy. He could hear the shaman speaking on two levels, but the levels kept shifting; Indy had the feeling he was trying to see through broken glasses.

Short Round didn't like the direction of this conversation one bit. "Bad news. You listen to Short Round, you live longer." He especially didn't like the interest Indy was showing in the subject. Evil was something you didn't play around with. Evil didn't care if you could shoot straight, or run fast.

The shaman continued. "They came from Palace and took Sivalinga from our village."

"Took what?" broke in Willie. She, too, was getting interested: there was a drama unfolding here, like a dark stage play. She had the sense she was being auditioned for a part.

"A stone," Indy explained. "A sacred stone from the shrine that protects the village."

"It is why Krishna brought you here," the shaman nodded.

Indy wanted to set him straight on that account, though. "No. We weren't brought here. Our plane crashed."

Short Round agreed with this assessment. He said "Boom!" and fluttered his fingers down into the palm of his other hand, to make the explanation more graphic for these simple people.

Indy clarified further. "We were sabotaged by—"

"No," stated the shaman, like a patient teacher to a dim pupil. "We pray to Krishna to help us find the stone. It was Krishna who made you fall from sky. So you *will* go to Pankot Palace and find Sivalinga and bring back to us."

Indiana started to object. But then he looked at the sad, pleading Chieftain, the starving peasants, the tortured elders, all watching him helplessly. And he looked, too, once more, into the deep unwavering eyes of the old shaman.

Darkness fell. They all rose; the Chieftain led the way to the edge of the village, accompanied by peasants, elders, and guests. Torches flared throughout the assemblage, like furied spirits. Dogs howled mournfully; the stars seemed far away.

They approached a house-sized boulder, with a small dome-shaped altar cut into it. Shorty walked close beside Indiana, confused and apprehensive.

"Indy, they made our plane crash?" he whispered. "To get you here?"

"It's just superstition, Shorty," he reassured the boy. "Just a ghost story. Don't worry about it."

Short Round wasn't reassured. He knew ghost stories—tales of mountain demons, and ancestral wandering spirits, stories his brothers had told him before the night they disappeared, stories he'd heard on the street after his family was all gone, after they themselves had been stolen away by thunder-goblins. Stories from shadowy alleyways, and the backs of bars. Stories that came to life at night, when the ghosts came out.

Shorty spoke a silent petition to the God of the Door of Ghosts, the deity who kept vagrant spirits from entering our world . . . or allowed them to pass.

When the group reached the carved niche, the shaman made a gesture of devotion. Short Round began climbing up the rockface to look into this primitive shrine—just to be sure there were no ghosts inside that might be a threat to Indy—but Indiana pulled him back down to earth, giving him a cautionary look.

"They took the Sivalinga from here?" Indy asked the Chief.

"Yes."

Indiana examined the little nook. It was empty, but an indentation at its base indicated the conical shape of the stone that once had lain there. The shape was familiar to him. "The stone, was it very smooth?"

"Yes," nodded the shaman.

"It was from the Sacred River?"

"Yes. Brought here long ago, before my father's father."

"With three lines across it." Indy could see it in his mind.

"Yes, that is right."

"Representing the three levels of the universe," Indy went on: the illusion of worldly matter; the reality of transcendental spirit; the oneness of all space, time, and substance. It was potent mythology; it vaunted potent talismans. "I've seen stones like the one you lost. But why would the Maharajah take this Sacred Stone from here?"

Willie was peering into the empty shrine over Indy's shoulder. Shorty held on to her leg.

The shaman spoke fiercely. "They say we must pray to their evil god. We say we will not." Firelight danced in the tearful mist that coated his eyes.

Willie spoke softly. "I don't understand how losing the rock could destroy the village."

The shaman was torn by the fullness of his emotion. He tried to speak, but could not find the words in English. Slowly he talked, in his own language, to give his heart some small measure of ease. "Sive linge nathi unata..."

Indy translated softly for the others. *"When the Sacred Stone was taken, the wells dried up. Then the river turned to sand."* He looked back at the shaman. "Idorayak?" he asked, meaning: "Drought?"

"Na!" the shaman denied. "Gos Kolan maha polawa..."

And again, Indiana translated the Hindi: *"Our crops were swallowed by the earth, and the animals lay down and turned to dust. One night there was a fire in the fields. The men went out to fight it. When they came back they heard the women crying in the darkness. Lamai."*

"Lamai," echoed Willie, intently following the words on Indy's lips in the light of the torches.

"The children," whispered Indy. "He said they stole their children."

The shaman walked to the edge of the torchlight and stared out into the darkness. Willie wanted to cry. Short Round felt a chill creep into his breast; he moved closer to Indy. Indy had no words.

The shaman gave a weighted sigh, returned to the circle of light, faced Indy. "You will find our children when you find Sivalinga."

Indy had to clear his throat before he could speak. "I'm sorry. But I don't know how I can help you." He didn't want to know. There was something deathly about all this. It felt like the edge of a maelstrom.

The shaman and the Chieftain stared keenly into Indiana's eyes, refusing to accept his denial. Theirs were the eyes of the village, the soul of a crumbling people.

Indy continued to protest. "The English authorities who control this area are the only ones who can help you."

"They do not listen," droned the Chieftain.

"I have friends in Delhi, and I will make sure they investigate this."

"No, you *will* go to Pankot," the shaman charged him. The old man repeated this over several times in his own tongue; with each monotone repetition, Indy felt his resistance dissolving, felt his will reforming in the way the banks of a river will change inexorably under the torrent of the monsoon and be the same river yet altered in its course.

The shaman continued speaking, still in the language of his people.

"What's he saying now?" Willie prompted.

Indy spoke hoarsely. "He says it was destined that I come here. He says I will know evil; evil already sees me here and knows I am coming. This is my destiny, and the future cannot be changed. He says he cannot see this future. It is my journey alone."

Short Round and Willie stared at Indy, in the thrall of the story.

Indy gazed, disturbed, at the shaman, each man dancing in the other man's eyes.

The three companions lay in their hut, trying to sleep, but could not sleep. Images haunted them: disappearing children, animals turning to dust, emptiness incarnate; red flames, black souls.

Indy had explored enough dark regions of the globe to know that every belief system had its own sphere of influence; every magic held sway in the provinces that spawned it. And magic was afoot here, exerting a power over him he could as yet ill define. Still, neither could he put it from his mind. He could only wrestle with it, in the shadows of his half-sleep.

Willie just wanted to leave. She hated this place—the dirt, the hungry farmers, the tense air. It was like just before a tornado, back home. Just before the roof fell in. She wished she could hail a taxi out of here.

Short Round had a bad feeling, a very bad feeling. These people were putting Indy under a spell, binding his spirit so his body would have to follow. Short Round had heard such stories from sailors who'd been to the Philippines or to Haiti; such stories rarely ended well. He would have to be constantly vigilant now, to protect Indy from inner threats as well as outer. He'd have to be more than a bodyguard now; he'd have to be a soul-guard.

Nor was the lady safe, he sensed. Ghosts nibbled her shadow. He could see them from the corner of his eyes; they vanished only if he turned his head to view them straight on. So Short Round would have to watch out for her, too. Otherwise, who would be Indy's wife in America, after they escaped this spooky, barren place?

He invoked Huan-t'ien, the Supreme Lord of the Dark Heaven, who lived in the northern sky and drove away evil spirits. Only after he'd done so could he finally go to sleep.

At last, Indiana, too, slept. In a dream, something came to him.

It came out of darkness, rushing headlong. Terror was at its core; branches tore at its face. Its breathing was heavy under the full moon. The wind moaned it along, it flew through the night out of the night's black nothing into Indy's sweating, sleeping brain. . . .

His eyes opened. What was it? He heard something; he was certain of it. Something running; crashing through the underbrush. Slowly, he sat up, listening.

Short Round and Willie slept near at hand. Something strange was happening, though. Indy sensed it. He stood, went to the door of the hut, walked outside.

The wind was rising; the moon, an ocherous coin. There: a crunch in the bushes over to the left. Indy turned. The branches rustled. Suddenly, out of the undergrowth, a child appeared, running straight toward him.

Indy squatted down; the child fell into his arms, unconscious. It was a boy of seven or eight, emaciated to the point of starvation, dressed in a few shredded rags. His back was marked by the lash.

Indiana called for help, carried the child into his hut, lay him down on the blanket. A few minutes later the elders were all crouched around. Yes, they said, this was a child of their village.

The shaman dripped a wet rag over the boy's forehead and into his mouth, then said a few words of healing. The child's eyes fluttered open. He looked around the room dazedly at all the strange and familiar faces that peered down at him—looked around the room until his gaze fell on Indiana.

The boy's arm moved weakly, lifted up, reached out to Indy and to no one else. Indy took the small hand in his own. He could see that the dark, delicate fingers were cut and bruised; they held something tightly. Gradually the child's fist relaxed; the fingers dropped something into Indy's hand.

The boy tried to whisper. Indiana leaned close to hear as the child's lips moved, almost inaudibly: "Sankara," he said.

His mother ran in; word had quickly reached her that it was her child. She kneeled down, took the boy in her arms, hugged him hard, choked back her sobs. Willie and Short Round looked on, wide-eyed and speechless.

Indy stood, staring at what the little boy had given him. It was a small, tattered piece of cloth, an old fragment of a miniature painting.

And Indiana recognized it.

"Sankara," he murmured.

4

Pankot Palace

Dawn came early.

Indy walked briskly across the village, getting last-minute instructions and pleas from the peasants who trotted alongside him to keep up with his pace. At the outskirts of town, two large elephants stood waiting.

Sajnu, the guide, was politely trying to drag Willie toward one of them. She was politely refusing.

"Damn it, Willie, get on! We've got to move out!"

Okay, okay, he's right; this is stupid, she thought. *We've got to go, and this is just a domestic animal. A large, unpredictable, occasionally ferocious, domestic animal. Besides, it's the only ride in town. Okay.* She hadn't gotten to where she'd gotten in life by being a shrinking violet. Then she wondered just where *had* she gotten. Mayapore, India. She didn't want to think about that too long, so she took a deep breath and let Sajnu help her up onto the back of the beast.

"Whoa! Easy, now. Nice elephant," she soothed, sitting rock-still on its shoulders, a cross between absolute self-control and impending terror on her face, her golden dress still in her hands.

Standing by the second elephant, Short Round watched Indy approach. He ran up to the doctor with a scrutable smile all over. "I ride with you, Indy?"

"Nope, you got a little surprise over there, Shorty."

Short Round ran behind the large lead elephant, to see a baby pachyderm being brought in. Just his size! He couldn't believe his incredible luck! What an adventure! What a nifty trunk! What a great pet!

"Oh, boy!" he shouted, and jumped up with a hand from the second guide. He knew just how to do it: he'd learned it all watching *Tarzan*. The elephants in that movie were great friends to Tarzan; so they would be to Short Round.

Jane was also a great friend to Tarzan. Short Round reflected on the ways in which Willie compared to Jane, with respect to men. He hoped Willie did better with Indy than she did with elephants.

Sajnu goaded Willie's animal over toward Short Round. She'd gotten over her initial fears, but was now twisting and shifting all over in a vain effort to find a satisfactory position on the animal's back. When her mount was even with Shorty's, the two guides began leading them out of town.

Willie relaxed enough for a moment to notice the grief-stricken look on many of the villagers' faces. Some even wept. It caught Willie short.

"This is the first time anybody ever cried when

I left," she confided to Short Round.

"They don't cry about you," he assured her. "They cry about the elephants leaving." That must be it: they were such great elephants!

"Figures," Willie admitted sullenly.

"They got no food to feed them. So they taking the elephants away to sell them. Indy said so."

Willie heard the third elephant behind her just then, and swiveled completely around on her own creature's back to see Indy lumbering over on his long-tusked bull.

"Willie, stop monkeying around on that thing," he scolded her.

Short Round giggled. "Lady, your brain is backwards. That way China; this way Pankot."

Pankot? she thought.

Indiana called down to Willie's guide: "Sajnu, imanadu."

And Sajnu yelled up at Willie, "Aiyo nona, oya pata nemei!" Then he yelled at her elephant.

"Wait a minute, wait a minute, I'm not comfortable yet," she shouted back. "Indiana, I can't go all the way to Delhi like this."

"We're not going to Delhi," Indiana said more quietly.

"Not going to Delhi!" she shrieked. Panic seized her. "Hey, wait a minute!" She looked down at the villagers in supplication. "Can't somebody take me to Delhi? I don't want to go to Pankot."

"All right, let's go," Indy called down to the guides. "I want to get there before tomorrow night."

Sajnu guided Willie's elephant; the beast lurched forward. The villagers waved at her fondly, and wished her great success, and blessed her for her courage.

"Indiana!" she hollered at the mastermind of this plot. "Damn it, why'd you change your mind? What did that kid tell you last night?"

For the time being, he disregarded her. The elephants moved off through the hordes of pitiful townspeople. In their midst, Indy saw the Chieftain and the old shaman, who brought his hands up to his forehead as the entourage rode past.

The going was slow but steady, bringing the distant hills closer with each passing hour. The countryside remained sparse here, though not nearly so desolate as it had been in the areas immediately surrounding the village. Tall grass became prevalent, along with short, scrubby trees. An occasional small mammal could be seen skittering out of harm's way.

Short Round was constantly discovering new things about his elephant. The fine, fuzzy hair that stuck straight up all over the top of its head was bristly as a blowfish; its skin was coarse everywhere but the underside of its trunk, which was smooth as a cow's udder; and if he scratched the bony knobs above its eyebrow, it would honk the most pleased and funny sound. It told him its name was, coincidentally, Big Short Round.

Willie had come to terms with her brute, in a manner of speaking, although the manner of speaking was too down and dirty to be called exactly the King's English. Nonetheless, they'd reached an uneasy truce, in which the elephant moved the way it wanted to and Willie enumerated all the uses she could think of for elephant glue.

By early afternoon the sun was enormous. They

trekked through areas that were increasingly ver-
dant, replete with banyan trees, climbing fig, leafy
ground cover, tepid streams. Increasingly muggy,
as well.

Willie looked down at herself in disgust. She still
wore Indy's baggy formal shirt, now all sticky with
heat, filthy with leaves and trail dust; his tuxedo
pants, nearly rubbed bare on the seat, it felt like;
and his white coat, tied around her waist. How could
she have sunk to this level? What had she ever done
to hurt anyone? She looked at her sequined gown,
all bunched up in her hands. Just yesterday she'd
been a real lady.

She pulled herself together all of a sudden. *Stop
it, Willie, stop it, stop it. Being a lady is all a state
of mind, and there's no reason on earth why I can't
be one right here on this Godforsaken lump of animal.*

She removed a small bottle of expensive French
perfume from an inner pocket of her once-beautiful
dress. And with great aplomb began to dab it behind
her ears.

It soon became evident, however, that she wasn't
the only one suffering from this heat. She looked
down at the beast between her legs and muttered,
"I think you need this more than me." So she leaned
forward and, with a sense of her own largesse,
dabbed some of the cologne behind the elephant's
ears. She had to lean close to reach down there,
though; the animal's smell was so overpowering,
Willie grimaced, swung around, and dumped half
the contents of her bottle over its back.

The elephant was outraged. It brought its trunk
back over its head, sniffed the foreign fragrance per-
functorily, and trumpeted in disgust.

Willie looked irked. "What are you complaining about? This is ritzy stuff."

The elephant only moaned, and kept on trudging.

Indy dozed recurrently throughout the day, while Short Round carried on an endless conversation with Big Short Round. By late afternoon, the terrain changed again; they passed into the lower jungles.

The surroundings here were lush, steamy. The canopy hung a hundred feet overhead, so thick that the sun barely sparkled through, making the air itself seem to take on a deep gold-green hue. Huge rubber trees abounded, draped with hanging moss and dangling lianas. Interspersed everywhere were exotic fruit trees, fern trees, palm, and willow.

A path did exist, but it was intermittent. Periodically one of the guides would have to clear away a fallen branch or cut back a tendril.

The place was full of sounds, too. Willie had never heard so many unknown calls: chirps, caws, growls, screams, and clackerings. Some of them gave her goose bumps. Once, something died out there: nothing else could have sounded so. It made her swear under her breath; she held on tighter than she liked to her elephant's rein. Sometimes, she reckoned, it was just plain hard to be a lady.

It was easy, however, to be a little boy. Short Round took in the sights and sounds as if they were all part of a grand new game, designed especially for him. He carried himself alternately like a king or a puppy dog—though he regularly looked over to check on Indy's whereabouts, never forgetting his first responsibility was still as number-one bodyguard.

There was thunder and lightning for a short time,

though no rain came. To Short Round this was a bad portent. It meant Lei-Kung (Lord of Thunders) and Tien-Mu (Mother of Lightnings) were fighting without cause. No good could come of such a quarrel. Lei-Kung was hideous to behold: owl-beaked, with talons on his blue, otherwise human body; he tended to hide in the clouds, beating his drum with a wooden mallet if anyone came near. Tien-Mu made lightning by flashing two mirrors; but when her mood was perverse, she would flash one at Lei-Kung, so he could see his own reflection and be appalled. Then he would beat his drum louder. But there was no rain to issue from the confrontation; only the dry anger of these two Ancient Ones.

Short Round made an invocation to the Celestial Ministry of Thunder and Wind, requesting a higher authority to intervene in the matter, whatever it was.

Ultimately the bickering ceased. Short Round remained cautious, however.

Once, spotting something on an overhanging branch, he stood precariously on the baby elephant's back to reach up and grab it. It was a globular fruit. He plucked it from its twig, then plopped back down onto his mount. He held it snugly between the knuckles of his first two fingers and the ball of his thumb, and gave his wrist a smart twisting motion several times. Lefty Grove.

"You come to America with me and we get job in the circus," he told Big Short. "You like that?" Ever since he'd seen the Charlie Chaplin film about the circus, Short Round had wanted to join.

The junior elephant's trunk curled back, took the fruit from Short Round's hand, and stuck it into its mouth with a joyful little slurp. Short Round understood this to mean that his elephant had appreciated the same movie.

They came to a shallow river. Sajnu called up to Indy; Indy nodded. Sajnu turned and led the procession up the wide, shin-deep stream: Shorty's elephant first, then Indy's, then Willie's. Thirty yards upstream, Shorty heard a strange noise, followed it aloft into the treetops.

"Indy, look!" he shouted.

Indy and Willie both looked up to see hundreds of huge winged creatures flapping across the dusky sky.

"What big birds," Willie commented. How interesting.

Sajnu said something to Indy, and the professor nodded. "Those aren't big birds," he told Willie. "Those are giant bats."

Short Round cringed. He'd seen *Dracula* twice, so he knew what bats could mean.

Willie shuddered too, instinctively crouching lower on her elephant. Unfortunately, this brought her closer (again) than her nose wanted to be. She made a face, mumbling, "Honey, this jungle heat is doing nothing for your allure," and poured the rest of her perfume on its neck.

The effect was instantly gratifying. It was the aroma of civilization; it evoked the memory of cabarets and rich benefactors and beautiful clothes and satin pillows. It made Willie positively glad to be alive, giant bats or no giant bats; and without another thought, she burst into loud, exuberant song:

"'In olden days a glimpse of stocking was looked on as something shocking; now, heaven knows, anything goes!'"

It took Indy by surprise to hear her singing like

that out here. Made him laugh; made him want to sing himself, suddenly, though he hardly knew any songs, and his voice was profoundly unmelodious. Nevertheless, he began to bellow: "'Oh, give me a home, where the buffalo roam, where the deer and the antelope play.'"

Short Round thought this was hysterical. A singing game in which everyone sang their favorite song as loudly as possible. Instantly he chimed in:

"'The golden sun is rising, shining in the green forest, shining through the city of Shanghai.'"

And Willie crooned louder: "'Good authors, too, who once knew better words, now only use four-letter words writing prose, anything goes.'"

"'Where seldom is heard a discouraging word, and the skies are not cloudy all day.'"

"'The city of Shanghai, I love the city, I love the sun.'"

"'The world's gone mad today, and good's bad today, and black's white today, and day's night today.'"

"'Home, home on the range.'"

Then Shorty joined in with Indy, because he loved that song, too: "'Where the deer and the antelope play.'"—except he was singing it in Chinese.

And they were all singing at the top of their cacophonous voices, to drown each other out, to celebrate the great good fortune of being alive and singing in this very moment of the universe.

Well, this was the last straw for Willie's elephant. First that horrible alien odor, now this agonizing squawking: the combination was simply intolerable. The animal stopped suddenly, dipped its trunk in the stream through which they were marching, sucked up about twenty gallons of water, curled its trunk backwards over its head, and gave Willie a sustained, pressurized hosing.

She flew off the critter's back, splashing down into the stream with an ignominious thump.

Short Round giggled uproariously, pointing down at her. "Very funny!" he said with glee. "Very funny all wet!"

It was the last straw for Willie as well, though. Like an overtired child slapped for playing too hard, she was caught between rage and tears of frustration. She was wet and dirty and hungry and taxed to the end of her rope, and this was the damn limit.

"I was happy in Shanghai," she seethed, letting her temper rise to its own level. "I had a little house, a garden; my friends were rich; I went to parties and rode in limousines. I hate being outside! I'm a singer; I'm not a camper! I could lose my voice!"

Short Round's eyes grew wide as he watched her. "Lady real mad," he concluded.

Indiana looked around where they were paused, judged the height of the declining sun, the depth of the encroaching gloom, and came to his own conclusion. "I think maybe we'll camp here."

He figured they were probably *all* getting a bit fatigued.

Sunset.

The three elephants submerged, chest deep in a wide spot in the river. Indy waded nearby, his shirt off, splashing water on the weary animals. Sajnu did the same from the other side.

Short Round played laughingly with the baby. The elephant would wrap him in its trunk, swing him in the air, flop him on its back. Then he'd dive in again, and when he resurfaced, the elephant would give him a shower. The two of them were of an age.

Thirty yards upstream, in a shady, recessed alcove, Willie was taking a leisurely swim. She dove to the cool bottom, turned slowly, went limp, resurfaced, wiped her hair from her eyes, backfloated, hummed contentedly, watched the patterns in the leaves overhead. She needed this.

Her life had turned upside down over the past two days. Things had been just peachy until this guy walked into the club, and then.... He wasn't so bad, really, she supposed—if you liked the type—but she didn't particularly think she wanted to elevate him to the category of Current Events.

For one thing, he was an academic, which meant, for all intents and purposes, broke. For another thing, although he was obviously infatuated with her, he never said anything nice, never went out of his way to cut her any slack, never empathized with her, and, in general, never acted like a gentleman. A thoroughly selfish, manipulative boor. So what good was he, she wondered.

Well, he *was* nice to the kid. That was one thing. Nobody had ever been nice to *her* when *she* was a kid, and it made her feel good to see this kid treated right. The starving kid in the village last night had really affected him, too; she'd seen that. So, okay, he was good with kids. What else?

Well, he *had* saved her hide when everything had gone to hell in the nightclub, and again in the crashing plane—though if he hadn't come along, it seemed unlikely any of that would have happened in the first place. Or maybe it would have. That's what karma was all about; these Indians loved to talk it to death. So did the Chinese, at some of the parties she used to go to.

71

Parties. They must be a thousand miles from the nearest party right now. *When every night the set that's smart is intrudin' in nudist parties in studios, anything goes.* His eyes, of course; that was his best feature. She wondered what they *really* looked like, up close.

She dove under again, letting the cool water relax her further, drain all the accumulated tension from her limbs. Oh, well, things would work out; they always did, if she just hung in there.

Imagine, though: a thousand miles away from the nearest pair of stockings.

Indiana wandered up the riverbank in his dripping trousers, checking on Willie, to make sure she was safe.

Not that she wouldn't be, of course. She was a lady with sand; that much was obvious. She'd been around the track, and she didn't always come up smelling like roses, but she always came up. She was just out of her element here, that's all. She was a city girl.

He wouldn't have ridden her so much if he hadn't thought she could take it. But he felt compelled to do it; she was such a royal pain at times. Still, you couldn't exactly blame a person for being a pain if they were so clearly hurting. Only did she have to be so vocal about it? He supposed that's why she was a singer.

Anyway, it was clear she needed to be cared for out here, and the poor thing obviously had a huge crush on him, so he thought he might as well check up on her, just make sure she didn't get carried off by mosquitoes.

He came upon her drying clothes spread out on

a tree limb hanging low over the water. A moment later, he saw Willie paddling around just beyond—completely, so to speak, unencumbered. The sight made his mouth go ever so slightly dry.

"Hey, Willie," he called. "I think you better get out now."

His sudden appearance startled her, but she quickly recovered her composure: this was a scenario she'd encountered hundreds of times. "Stark naked?" she said evenly. "You wish."

"C'mon, time to dry off."

"Dry up," she countered. "Dr. Jones, if you're trying to seduce me, this is a very primitive approach."

Try to be a nice guy, and look where it gets you. "Me seduce *you*? Honey, you're the one who took your clothes off." He shrugged with monumental disinterest. "I just came over to remind you that you never know what else might be in that water."

Even though they were out in the middle of nowhere, maybe ten thousand miles from Cole Porter, Willie felt sure this was extremely familiar territory. "Somehow I feel safer in here," she smiled.

"Suit yourself," he said with a gesture of supreme indifference.

He turned and walked back to camp, just the slightest bit miffed.

While she, for all her urbane wit, found herself inexplicably peeved he hadn't stayed longer.

Night came quickly on the forest. The campfire gave a warm, orange light, but immediately outside its friendly glimmer, the shadows were black, enveloping, unyielding.

Sajnu was feeding the elephants; the other guides

talked quietly among themselves. Willie, wrapped in a blanket, was wringing out her damp clothing by the fire; in this humid hothouse, it wasn't drying well. She half-intentionally dribbled water on Indy's back as he sat playing poker with Short Round, then took it all over to a peripheral low branch, to hang it out to dry overnight.

Indiana gave a look, but didn't say anything, only continued playing cards.

"What you got?" Short Round asked seriously.

"Two sixes."

"Three aces. I win." The boy grinned. "Two more games. I have all your money."

Shorty discarded; Indy dealt.

Willie looked over from unfolding her clothes along the branch. "Where'd you find your little bodyguard?" she asked Indy.

"I didn't find him. I caught him," Jones replied, picking up his cards.

"What?" she said, repositioning some of the larger pieces.

"His parents were killed when they bombed Shanghai. Shorty's been on the street since the age of four. I caught him trying to pick my pocket."

Willie went for the final piece of clothing on the branch beneath her. She unfolded a giant bat.

She let go with a scream that turned everyone's head except Indy, who simply winced. Leaping back from the flapping, clawing, hissing bat, she turned into a large fern, only to come face to face with a vicious baboon. Its snout was pink and purple; it snarled malevolently at Willie's intrusion.

She shrieked again, scaring the baboon off—and backed directly into a dark rock on which a large iguana perched. It snapped at her.

Short Round wasn't particularly worried, once the bat flew away—though he did offer a dollar (on account) to the God of the Door of Ghosts once more, as well as to Dr. Van Helsing and all the other guardians against Dracula.

Willie, unfortunately, had no such spiritual protectors. All she had were her worst suspicions about the Great Outdoors being confirmed.

In the ensuing frenzy, Indiana accidentally dealt himself a fourth card. Short Round noticed the misdeal and started doing a slow burn.

Willie began a frenetic, exhaustive examination of the environs of the campsite, punctuated by numerous squeals and yelps.

"The trouble with her," Indy grumbled, "is the noise." He tried to concentrate on his cards.

"I take two," Short Round said guardedly.

Indy nodded. "Three for me."

"Hey, you take four," Shorty protested.

"No, I did not take four." Indy was indignant.

"Dr. Jones cheat," he accused.

"I didn't take any but I think you stole a card," Indy countered.

Willie whooped at another rustling. She kicked an empty bush.

"You owe me ten cents," Shorty demanded. "You pay money. You pay now."

Indy disgustedly threw down his cards. "I don't want to play anymore."

"Me neither."

"And I'm *not* teaching you anymore."

"I don't care. You cheat. I quit." He picked up the cards and stalked off, muttering in Chinese.

Willie backed her way over to Indiana, still sitting by the fire. She was looking wildly in all directions.

"We're completely surrounded!" she choked. "This whole place is crawling with living things." She shivered.

"That's why it's called the jungle," he said drolly.

"What else is out there?" she whispered.

He looked at her, smiled. *Willie*. That was a funny name. He let it roll off his tongue. "Willie. Willie. Is that short for something?"

She stiffened a bit; she would not be ridiculed. "Willie is my professional name—Indiana." She put the emphasis on the *ana*.

Short Round, still sulking near his elephant, came to Indy's defense. "Hey, lady, you call him *Dr. Jones*." She was getting a little too familiar for someone Short Round had not yet officially sanctioned to be the object of Indy's courtship.

Willie and Indy both smiled. He flicked a dime over to Shorty, to make peace, then watched Willie again. "That's *my* professional name." He turned a little toward her. "So how'd you end up in Shanghai?"

"My singing career got run over by the Depression," she moped. "Some big ape convinced me a girl could go places in the Orient."

He spread out a blanket near the fire, lay down on it. "Show business, eh? Any other ambitions?"

A terrible scream issued from the jungle. Feral, deathly. Willie tightened, drew closer to the blaze.

"Staying alive till morning," she groaned.

"And after that?"

She smiled inwardly. "I'm going to latch onto a good-looking, incredibly rich prince."

"I'd like to dig up one of those myself," he agreed. "Maybe we do have something in common."

"Huh?"

"I like my princes rich and dead, and buried for a couple of thousand years. Fortune and glory. You know what I mean." He began carefully unfolding a piece of cloth he'd removed from his pocket—the fragment the child had given him last night in Mayapore.

Willie sat beside him, staring at it. "Is that why you're dragging us off to this deserted palace? Fortune and glory?"

He showed her the relic. "This is a piece of an old manuscript. This pictograph represents Sankara, a priest. It's hundreds of years old. Gently, gently."

She took it from him to inspect more closely. It was a crude rendering, painted in faded reds, golds, blues. It was fascinating.

Willie touched its history, its arcane wisdom. Shorty wandered over to look, too; they were both getting genuinely interested, affected by Indy's tone of reverence. It even drew the baby elephant's attention; he sidled over beside Willie, placing his trunk on her shoulder.

She jumped, then brushed the trunk away impatiently, returning her attention to the pictograph. "Is this some kind of writing?"

"Yeah, it's Sanskrit," said Indy. "It's part of the legend of Sankara. He climbs Mount Kalisa, where he meets Shiva, the Hindu god."

The elephant hung its trunk on Willie's shoulder again; again, she swatted it off. "Cut it out," she snapped. Then to Indy, "That's Shiva, huh? So what's he handing the priest?"

"Rocks. He told him to go forth and combat the evil, and to help him, he gave him five sacred stones that had magical properties."

The elephant nudged Willie again. Her patience was fast running out. "Magic rocks. My grandfather spent his entire life with a rabbit in his pocket and pigeons up his sleeves, and made a lot of children happy, and died a very poor man. Magic rocks. Fortune and glory. Good night, Dr. Jones." She handed him back the cloth and walked to the edge of the clearing, where she put down her blanket.

"Where are you going?" asked Indy. "I'd sleep closer. For safety's sake." He watched her with mixed feelings. She was starting to get under his skin. He tried not looking at her, but that somehow made things worse.

Willie likewise refused to return his glance. Couldn't he be honest about his feelings, for crying out loud? She just didn't trust men who weren't straightforward about what they wanted. "Dr. Jones, I think I'd be safer sleeping with a snake."

At that moment, a giant python descended from the tree behind her; it curled over her shoulder. Short Round was aghast. Indy was more than that: Indy was frozen-stone-petrified of snakes. He didn't know why, he didn't care why. He only knew that of all the creatures that ever existed, might exist, or would never exist, snakes alone made him sweat bullets, shiver, want to run.

Willie, however, thought this was still the baby elephant. Losing all patience, she reached up behind her without looking, grabbed the snake by the neck, and hurled it backwards. "I said, cut it out!"

Indy inched a slow retreat, staring, sweating. Willie bent over to straighten her blanket. The snake slithered away.

"I hate this jungle," Willie muttered. "I hate that elephant. I hate these accommodations."

Nearby, unseen, a Bengal tiger cut a silent path through the thicket and was gone. Indy sat on a rock for a few seconds, took a couple of deep breaths; then got up and started loading more wood on the fire.

A lot more wood.

They broke camp early the next morning, to try to make time before the heat of the day. Tropical winds rippled the uppermost vines as the elephants plowed on through the thick of it. The air was teeming with sounds of animal life, though it didn't seem nearly so ominous now that night had lifted. It reminded Willie of a large, poorly kept zoo.

Short Round was back to conversing with Big Short Round, increasingly convinced that the spirit of his lost brother Chu, snagged on the Wheel of Transmigration, had been deposited in the body of this large baby. For one thing, Chu had himself been of the rotund persuasion, a proclivity well invested in an incarnation like the elephant; for another, Chu was always in excellent good humor, as was this beast. Lastly, Chu's nickname had been Buddha, not only for his portliness and disposition, but because of the substantial size of his earlobes—and of course the size of the young elephant's ears need hardly be mentioned.

So Short Round discussed things with Big Short Round that only Chu could have understood or cared about—family matters, certain toys of disputed ownership, apologies for long-dormant squabbles over such heated concerns as whether Jimmy Foxx or Lou Gehrig was the stronger clean-up batter—and to Shorty's great relief, the elephant put his mind at ease on all of these issues.

They were just on to New Business, speculating about all the things they would see in America when they joined the circus together, when they came over a rise, and saw, far in the distance, the palace.

Resplendent, almost iridescent white alabaster, it perched on the carpeted jungle crest like a carved pearl on a sea of green jade.

"Indy, look!" gasped Short Round.

"That's Pankot," he nodded.

They all stared in silence a full minute; then headed on.

It was well after lunchtime before they reached the base of the foothills that rose finally to the palace. They were about to enter the first low pass when Sajnu stopped the elephants with a command and ran forward.

"Navath thana." His voice held fear.

Indy jumped down off his mount and walked ahead to join the guide. As he approached, he could see that Sajnu was staring at something, chattering frantically: "Winasayak. Maha winasayak." *A calamity, a great calamity.*

Indy tapped him on the shoulder; he ran back to the other guides, gibbering away. Indy now saw what had affected him so.

It was a small statue guarding the path, a goddess with eight arms. A malign deity, wearing a carved necklace of small human heads. Each of her hands dangled another head by the hair. She scowled demonically.

It was further adorned with ritual objects: leaves, dead birds, rodents, turtles. Around its waist was a bandolier of real, pierced human fingers.

Indy walked back to the group as Willie and Short Round were dismounting.

"Why are we stopping here?" asked Willie.

"What you look at, Indy?" said Short Round. Some treasure, maybe, for Chao-pao to discover.

Indy was talking to the agitated guides, though. Sajnu just kept shaking his head, turning the elephants around. "Aney behe mahattaya," he was saying. The guides began quickly driving the elephants away.

This rather distressed Willie. She ran after them a few steps, shouting. "No, no, no! Indy, they're stealing our rides!"

"From here on, we walk," said Indy. It was no use forcing natives to go where they were afraid to go; inevitably, things got worse.

"No!" she pouted. After all that aggravation yesterday, she was just starting to get used to the big ugly brutes.

Short Round watched the elephants trudging away. His big round friend turned its head to look back.

"Baby elephant!" Shorty called out. Could it be that after all these years, his beloved brother Chu had returned, only to stay for two days, then leave again? Wait! No fair! What about the circus?

But maybe he'd just come back to straighten out the differences between them that had been left unresolved years before in Shanghai. Maybe now that everything was settled amicably, it was time for Chu to leave again. This was hard for Short Round to accept, or even fathom, but it seemed to be so. For wasn't the reborn Chu smiling now as he bid farewell?

Short Round waved at the lost, found soul. His little pal trumpeted, and flapped his ears, and waved his trunk and lumbered off. Short Round tried very hard not to cry.

Indy walked back up to the idol. He studied it closely.

Short Round called up to him. "Dr. Jones, what you looking at?" Treasure was small consolation for a twice-lost brother, but it was some.

"Don't come up here," Indy called back. He didn't want them to see this, especially Short Round. It was a wicked totem, full of occult power. At best, it would cause horrible dreams; at worst...

Indy didn't think it served any purpose to expose Short Round to such depravity—or to expose Willie, for that matter, for he was beginning to feel a bit protective toward her, as well.

He stood and returned to his waiting friends. "We'll walk from here."

By late afternoon they came to a rock-paved road that ran along a high stone wall. Willie limped along a few yards behind the others, carrying her high-heels, sweating, disheveled, grumbling. "...shot at, fallen out of a plane, nearly drowned, chomped at by an iguana, attacked by a bat; I smell like an elephant..." Suddenly, feeling as though she couldn't take another step, she shouted at their backs: "I tell you, I'm not going to make it!"

Indiana stopped, walked back to Willie, was about to make a comment—something pithy, or sarcastic, or pointed—when, as in the first moment they'd met, their eyes came together. Something he saw there—lost, quiet at the end of the noise—stopped him. And something *she* saw, at least momentarily, brought her quiet to the surface.

Without a word, he picked her up in his arms, started carrying her the remaining distance. She was surprised, and puzzled—though not displeased.

"Any more complaints?" Indiana asked.

She smiled faintly. "Yeah. I wish you'd thought of this sooner." It didn't feel so bad at all.

Short Round rolled his eyes to the heavens. He'd seen Gable do that in *It Happened One Night*. He thought it was dumb in the movie; he thought it was dumb now.

Indy carried her all the way up the road along the wall, until they reached the large front gate. Here he put her down, gently smoothed her collar back in place. "Well, no permanent damage." He smiled.

She straightened herself, turned around, and for the first time saw Pankot Palace up close. She whistled.

It was magnificent, sprawling. An extravagant mixture of Moghul and Rajput styles, it reflected the dying sun with a bloody, opalescent hue.

The three travelers started slowly across a marble bridge toward the main entrance.

5

The Surprise in the Bedroom

Palace guards stood lining the bridge along both sides.

Bearded, black-turbaned, and beribboned, with scimitars in their belts and lances at their sides, they snapped to attention in sequence as the threesome passed. It made Willie jump at first, but she quickly grew to enjoy the attention. Her carriage improved; she assumed an air of grace appropriate to someone of her stature. She only wished she'd thought to put on her shoes before she'd come in.

They passed under a dark archway, into a glittering courtyard. Quartz and marble walls, lapis lazuli minarets, arching windows with gilt facades...like an opulent mausoleum. And just as deserted.

"Hello?" shouted Indy. His voice echoed from the somewhat foreboding walls.

Three enormous Rajput guards appeared silently at the opposite side of the courtyards. They did not look as deferential as the first platoon.

"Hi," Willie said to them, placating. The only response was her own echo.

A few moments later, between the guards, down the marble steps of the expansive entryway, stepped a tall, bespectacled, severe-looking Indian man dressed in a white English suit. He looked courteously, but suspiciously, at the woozy beauty dressed in a man's wrinkled tuxedo who carried her shoes and gown; the dirty Chinese boy wearing the American baseball cap; the Caucasian ruffian with a squint and a bullwhip.

His name was Chattar Lal.

He walked forward with a bureaucrat's briskness, to appraise the visitors more closely. Their appearance did not improve with proximity. "I would say you look rather lost." He smiled disdainfully. "But then I cannot imagine where in the world the three of you would look at home."

Indiana smiled his best, even, I'm-right-where-I-should-be-no-matter-where-I-am, American smile. "Lost? No, we're not lost. We're on our way to Delhi. This is Miss Scott, and this is Mr. Round. My name is Indiana Jones."

Chattar Lal was taken aback. "*Dr*. Jones? The eminent archaeologist?"

Willie sneered without rancor. "Hard to believe, isn't it?"

Chattar Lal went on. "I remember first hearing your name when I was studying at Oxford. I am Chattar Lal, Prime Minister for His Highness the Maharajah of Pankot." He bowed to do them honor. "Welcome to Pankot Palace."

He accompanied them through the central foyer, down pillared marble halls, past dazzling interiors, inlaid with mirror and semiprecious stones, ivory fountains, intricate tapestries.

Willie gazed in awe at the ornate splendor. Down the next corridor they passed the portraits, hanging chronologically, of the Pankot Princes. The faces were variously dissipated, elegant, evil, vapid, aged, ageless.

Willie whispered to Short Round as they went by each one. "How'd you like to run into *him* in a dark alley? That one's kind of cute. I could see myself married to a prince like that. Princess Willie."

Ahead of them, Chattar Lal questioned Indy in a tone midway between curiosity and mistrust. "The plane crash and your journey here sound...most incredible."

Willie heard that. "You should've been there," she cracked.

Indy sounded earnest. "We'd appreciate it if the Maharajah would let us stay tonight. We'll be on our way in the morning." Right after a little covert inspection tour.

"I am only his humble servant"—Chattar Lal bent his head obsequiously—"but the Maharajah usually listens to my advice."

"Is that him?" Willie asked. They'd come to the last picture in the row of portraits that lined the wall. Willie stopped and stared in frank disappointment at the immensely corpulent, aged Rajput prince. "He's not exactly what we call a spring chicken," she sighed.

"No, no," advised Chattar Lal, "that is Shafi Singh, the present Maharajah's late father."

"Oh, good," Willie brightened up some. "And

maybe the present Maharajah is a little *younger*? And thinner?"

Two female servants materialized from a side door and bowed.

Chattar Lal nodded to Willie. "They will escort you to your rooms now. You will be provided with fresh clothes. Tonight you will be dining with His Highness."

"Dinner?" beamed Willie. "And with a prince? Hey, my luck is changing." Until she caught sight of herself in a piece of decorative mirror. "But look at me. Oh, my God, I've got to get ready." To hook a prince, the correct bait was essential. She hurried off with one of the servants.

To Indiana, Chattar Lal offered a cool smile. "Eight o'clock in the Pleasure Pavilion, Dr. Jones."

They both bowed, each less deeply than the other.

An extraordinary golden dome rose above elaborate gardens. The night air was perfumed with jasmine, hyacinth, coriander, rose. The strains of sitar, tambour, and flute wafted on the torchlit breeze. The Pleasure Pavilion was aglow.

Rich court ministers and Indian merchants, decked out in their formal Rajput finery, mingled on the paths, trading innuendo and promise of booty for court favor and imagined privilege. Into this net of palace intrigue strode Indiana Jones with his bodyguard, Short Round.

Indy wore his traditional professorial raiment: tweed jacket, bow tie, round eyeglasses; his pants and shirt had been freshly cleaned by palace servants. He'd decided to keep his three-day growth of beard intact: he wanted to look rough and ready to this weird Prime Minister—and besides, he didn't want Willie to think he was trying to impress her. Short Round, too, was clean, though he'd refused to change clothes or remove his cap.

"Look around, Shorty," said Indiana. "You like to have a place like this someday?"

"Sure," said Short Round.

"Wrong," said Indy. "It's beautiful, okay, but it reeks of corruption. Smell it?"

Short Round sniffed the air. "I ... think so." There *was* a peculiar pungence to the air, like a too-sweet incense.

"Attaboy," nodded Indy. The kid had enough disadvantages without hooking him on this kind of wealth. "It looks good. I'll admit that. And it might be a nice place to visit, but you wouldn't want to live here."

"I live in America," Short Round agreed.

"Take that carved ivory sundial, over there, for example." He wished he *could* take it, all the way back to the university—it was a prime specimen of Tamil craftwork—but that wasn't the point he was trying to make. "It was clearly stolen from a different kingdom, purely for the aggrandizement of this palace."

Short Round nodded. "Just like us: they find new home for things."

Indy cleared his throat. "I don't think exactly just like us, Shorty."

Short Round was momentarily confused, but then he thought he saw what Indy was getting at. "Ah: these mans can't spell!"

"Right," said Indy. He decided to leave it at that, for the time being. "They can't spell."

"I think they know numbers pretty good, though,"

Short Round figured; anybody this rich had to at least be able to count money.

Indy smiled at his pal. "You got good eyes, kid."

They let their good eyes wander over the porcelain tiles, jade facades, fluted pillars.

As the hangers-on and functionaries began filing in, Chattar Lal approached. With him was a British cavalry captain, in full regalia.

Chattar Lal made the introductions. "We are fortunate tonight to have so many *unexpected* guests. This is Captain Phillip Blumburtt."

Blumburtt bowed to Shorty and Indiana. He was a proper gentleman, perhaps sixty, mustachioed, balding, wearing four medals across the chest of his dress uniform.

Indy shook his head. "Hello. I saw your troops come in at sunset."

"Just a routine inspection tour," he assured them all politely.

"The British worry so about their Empire." Chattar Lal tried to sound warm.

"Looks like you've got a pretty nice little empire here to worry about," smiled Indy.

As the four of them stood there admiring the architecture, Willie entered the gardens from a separate path. Indiana admired her architecture as well.

She looked stunning. Washed and made-up, she'd been lent a royal bone-colored silk sari, slightly westernized with a low V neckline and brocade borders. In her hair draped a diamond-and-pearl tiara; golden hoop earrings set off her face; an ornate gem-studded necklace sat, dazzling, across her chest; over her head was the finest silk veil.

It was truly a transformation.

"You look like a princess," said Indy.

As far as she could remember, this was the first nice thing he'd ever said to her. She nearly blushed.

Blumburtt and Lal made similarly complimentary remarks. The Prime Minister then noted that the dinner would soon begin, and led the way toward the dining hall. Willie was about to accompany him when Indy held her back a few steps.

"Don't look *too* anxious," he advised. "Your mouth is watering."

"I think it *is* sort of like being in heaven," she confessed. "Imagine, a real prince. My best before this was a provincial duke."

They crossed the gardens to the inner pavilion, Willie on Indy's arm. Her eyes were like a kid's at Christmas.

Short Round lagged several paces behind just to watch them. Lovely, stately, devoted, charmed. They were his idealized parents, at that moment, and he their faithful son. Pausing briefly, he sent off a simple prayer to his favorite stellar divinities—the Star of Happiness, the Star of Dignities, the Star of Longevity—asking that this moment be noted in the Celestial Archives so it could be later reproduced upon request.

Prayer finished, he caught up with them at a trot, falling quickly into step.

They entered the dining hall. Massive granite columns supported the rococo ceiling. Alabaster horses danced in bas-relief along the walls. The floor was marble and ebony. Crystal chandeliers refracted candlelight to every corner. In the center of the room a long, low table had place settings for twenty, marked by solid gold plates and cups. Bejeweled guards stood at rigid attention beside the doorway. Indy and company walked in.

Off to the side, drums and strings wove an exotic melody as a sparsely dressed dancing girl spun to the ecstasy of her muse. Indiana gave her the once-over, smiling appreciatively. "I've always had a weakness for folk dancing."

Willie nodded to the dancer, half-snide, half-encouraging. "Keep hoofin', kid; look where it got me." She gave Jones a disparaging glance, then quickened her stride to catch up to the Prime Minister." "Oh, Mr. Lal." Willie affected her most conversational tone. "What do you call the Maharajah's wife?"

"His Highness has not yet taken a wife," Chattar Lal demurred.

Willie beamed. "No? Well, I guess he just hasn't met the right woman."

As Willie entered into more intricate levels of small talk with the prime minister, Indiana wandered over to a far wall where numerous bronze statues and outré devotional objects were on display. One strange clay figurine attracted his attention right away. He picked it up to examine it as Blumburtt walked over to join him.

Blumburtt grimaced when he saw the small, strange doll. "Charming. What is it?"

"It's called a Krtya," said Indy. "It's like the voodoo dolls of West Africa. The Krtya represents your enemy—and gives you complete power over him."

"Lot of mumbo jumbo," Blumburtt blustered.

Indiana took an even tone. "You British think you rule India. You don't, though. The old gods still do." He'd had a sense of that when he saw the little statue that guarded the path to the palace. This Krtya doll only reinforced his impression.

Blumburtt looked sour. Indy put down the doll. Willie ran over, all excited from her chat with the Prime Minister.

"You know, the Maharajah is positively *swimming* in money." She flushed. "Maybe coming here wasn't such a bad idea after all."

Blumburtt arched his eyebrows at her with the gravest sort of misgivings. Indy merely smiled.

A drum boomed sonorously from the musicians' dais.

"I believe we're being called to dinner," Captain Blumburtt said, showing some relief.

"Finally!" Willie exclaimed. Blumburtt moved to separate himself from these people as quickly as possible.

Indiana took Willie's arm, and escorted her to table.

As the drum continued beating, the assembled guests took their places standing beside floor pillows that surrounded the low banquet table. Only the head of the table remained empty. Indiana was placed to its right, beside Captain Blumburtt; Willie and Shorty stood opposite them, to the left of the seat of honor.

Chattar Lal strolled over to the corner, near Willie, clapped his hands twice, and made an announcement, first in Hindi, then in English: "His Supreme Highness, guardian of Rajput tradition, the Maharajah of Pankot, Zalim Singh."

All eyes focused on two detailed, solid silver doors that were closed some ten feet behind the Prime

Minister. At once, the doors opened; across the threshold strode the Maharajah Zalim Singh. Everyone in the room bowed.

Indy saw Willie looking up from her obeisant position; saw her jaw literally fall open. He looked from her face to that of the entering monarch: Zalim Singh was only thirteen years old.

"That's the Maharajah?" she whispered. "That kid?" Never had disappointment weighed more heavily on a human face.

"Maybe he likes older women," suggested Indy.

Zalim Singh walked to the head of the table. He was outfitted in a long robe of gold and silver brocade, festooned with diamonds, rubies, emeralds, pearls. His turban was similarly jewel-encrusted, topped with a diadem in the shape of a spraying fountain. He was further adorned with earrings, finger rings, toe rings. His face had that pre-adolescent delicate softness about it: no wrinkles, no hair, puffed out to the barest sulk by the last vestiges of baby fat. Actually he looked quite feminine. And actually quite beautiful.

He gazed imperiously at the crowd...until his gaze fell upon Short Round. Short Round was not bowing.

Short Round was standing there in his baseball cap, chewing gum, glaring antagonistically at this kid who seemed to think he was some kind of bigshot.

Natural enemies.

Indy sent Short Round a withering look across the table, and though Shorty did *not* wither, he *did* bow. But he was bowing for Indy, he told himself, not for this haughty wimp.

The Maharajah finally sat down on his golden pillow. At a nod, the guests took their seats on the floor, reclining against cushions of their own.

Indy smiled sympathetically at Willie, her dreams of monarchy evaporated. "Cheer up," he consoled her. "You lost your prince, but dinner's on the way."

It was just what she needed to hear. Her crestfallen features became salivary. "I've never been so hungry in all my life."

Servants appeared with silver platters of steaming food. Willie closed her eyes a moment, savoring the aromas that filled her nostrils. When she opened them again, the first course sat before her: an entire roasted boar, arrows piercing its back and bloated stomach, tiny fetal boars impaled on the shafts, a rafter of broiled baby boars suckling on their well-cooked mother's teats.

Willie grimaced in amazement. "My God, it's sort of gruesome, isn't it?"

Indiana furrowed his brow. It seemed rather odd, at best. Hindus didn't eat meat. He glanced at Blumburtt, who seemed equally puzzled. Willie continued to stare at her food.

The young Maharajah leaned over to whisper something to Chattar Lal, on his left. The Prime Minister nodded, and addressed the group.

"His Highness wants me to welcome his visitors. Especially the renowned Dr. Jones from America."

Indy tipped his head slightly toward the little prince. "We are honored to be here."

A small pet monkey jumped up on Short Round's shoulder, stole a flower off the plate, chattered gaily. Short Round giggled. The monkey took his cap; he took it back. They shook hands, whispered secrets, played with the flower petals, like rowdy siblings at a family affair.

Willie just kept staring at the roast boar, skewered on its own children.

Indiana conversed neutrally with Chattar Lal. "I had a question, Mr. Prime Minister. I was examining some of the Maharajah's artifacts—"

"A fine collection of very old pieces, don't you think?"

"I'm not sure all the pieces are that old. Some were carved recently, I think. They look like images used by the Thuggees to worship the goddess Kali."

At the mention of the word *Thuggee*, the entire table quieted. As if a taboo had been broken, or some inexcusable social transgression committed, all the Indians stared at Jones.

Chattar Lal made an effort to be civil, though his manner was cold. "That is not possible, Dr. Jones."

"Well, I seem to remember that this province, perhaps this area, was a center of activity for the Thuggee." He seemed to have hit a nerve. From the reaction generated, he sensed it would be a useful line to pursue.

Blumburtt entered the conversation now. "Oh, the Thuggee. Marvelous brutes. Went about strangling travelers. Come to think of it, it *was* in this province. Brought to an end by a British serving officer, a major—"

"Sleeman," interjected Indiana. "Major William Sleeman."

"That's the fellow," Blumburtt concurred.

"He actually penetrated the cult and apprehended its leaders," Indy went on. "1830, I believe. Courageous man."

"You have a marvelous recall of past events." Chattar Lal spoke with growing interest.

"It's my trade," acknowledged Indy.

"Dr. Jones," the Prime Minister pressed, "you know very well that the Thuggee cult has been dead for nearly a century."

Blumburtt agreed. "Of course they have. The Thuggees were an obscenity that worshipped Kali with human sacrifices. The British army did away with them nicely."

A second platter was placed on the table by servants: steaming poached boa constrictor, with a garnish of fried ants. One of the servants slit the huge snake down the middle, exposing a mass of squirming, live baby eels inside.

Willie turned quite pale.

The merchant to her left chortled with satisfaction. "Ah! Snake Surprise!"

"What's the surprise?" Willie drooped. She was distinctly less hungry than she had been.

Indiana was pressing his dialogue with Chattar Lal. "I suppose stories of the Thuggees die hard." Especially when they had some basis for being perpetuated.

"There are *no* stories anymore." The Prime Minister begged to differ.

"Well, I don't know about that." Indy shook his head pleasantly. "We came here from a small village, and the peasants there told us that the Pankot Palace was growing powerful again, because of some ancient evil."

"These stories are just fear and folklore," Lal sneered.

"But then," Indy continued, "as I approached the palace, I found a small shrine. It contained a statue of the goddess Kali, the goddess of death, destruction, and chaos."

Zalim Singh and his prime minister exchanged a glance. Indiana noted the exchange. Chattar Lal composed himself before answering. "Ah, yes. We played there as children. My father always warned me not to let Kali take my Atman, or soul, as you say. But I remember no evil. I only recall the luxury of being young. And the love of my family and pets. Village rumors, Dr. Jones. They're just fear and folklore. You're beginning to worry Captain Blumburtt, I expect." His face was a mask.

"Not worried, Mr. Prime Minister," denied the jovial Blumburtt. "Just interested."

Short Round went back to playing with his little monkey friend. He didn't like this scary conversation. He hoped Huan-t'ien, Supreme Lord of the Dark Heaven, was keeping an eye on things down here.

But as if the talk weren't bad enough for Willie—human sacrifices, indeed—this food was unbelievable. And just when she was wondering about eating a flower, she looked up to see a servant lean over her shoulder and place a six-inch-long baked black beetle on her plate.

She whimpered quietly as she watched the fat merchant next to her lift a similar shiny, giant, grotesque insect off his dish and crack it in two. At which point he enthusiastically sucked the gooey innards out.

Willie turned even paler. Shimmering lights wiggled in her vision.

The merchant looked at her dubiously. "But you're not eating!"

She smiled weakly. "I, uh, had bugs for lunch."

Always be polite when dining with a Maharajah.

Meanwhile, the uneasy banter continued near the head of the table.

"You know," Indiana was saying, "the villagers also claimed that Pankot Palace took something from them."

"Dr. Jones." Chattar Lal's voice had become thick. "In our country a guest does not usually insult his host."

"Sorry," said Indiana. "I thought we were just talking about folklore." He kept his tone innocent, conversational, but his insinuations were clear to the people who feared them.

"What was it they claimed was stolen?" asked Blumburtt officiously. Thievery: now that was a different matter; that fell squarely within his purview.

"A sacred rock," said Indiana.

"Ha!" barked the Prime Minister. "There, you see, Captain—a rock!"

They all laughed uncomfortably.

Willie could concentrate only on the sight and sound of a dozen dinner guests breaking open these horrible mammoth beetles, then sucking out the insides. She leaned over to Short Round, who was teaching baseball signs to the monkey.

"Give me your hat," she rasped.

"What for?" he asked suspiciously.

"I'm going to puke in it."

A servant came forward to her side to offer assistance. Willie smiled at him as well as she could; she was nothing if not a trouper. "Listen, do you have something, you know, simple—like soup, or something?"

The servant bowed, left, and returned almost immediately with a covered bowl. He placed it in front of her, removed the cover. It was soup. Some kind of chicken base, it smelled like. With a dozen eyeballs floating in it.

The merchant nodded approvingly at Willie's choice. "Looks delicious!" he exclaimed.

Tears began to run down Willie's cheeks.

Indiana was still pushing Chattar Lal. "I was dubious myself, at first. Then something connected: the village's rock and the old legend of the Sankara Stone."

Chattar Lal was obviously having difficulty controlling his anger. "Dr. Jones, we are all vulnerable to vicious rumors. I seem to remember that in Honduras you were accused of being a graverobber rather than an archaeologist."

Indy shrugged. "The newspapers exaggerated the incident."

"And didn't the Sultan of Madagascar threaten to cut your head off if you ever returned to his country?" Chattar Lal suggested.

Indy remembered the Sultan well. "It wasn't my head," he mumbled.

"Then your *hands*, perhaps." By the gleam in his eye it seemed clear that the Prime Minister knew precisely what body parts had been threatened with extinction.

"No, not my hand," Indy backed off, a bit embarrassed. "It was my . . . it was my misunderstanding."

"Exactly what we have here, Dr. Jones." Lal sat back with a smile. "A misunderstanding."

The Maharajah suddenly coughed and, for the first time, spoke. "I have heard the terrible stories of the evil Thuggee cult."

His words silenced the table, as if it were a great

surprise for him to offer an opinion about anything.

"I thought the stories were told to frighten children," he went on. "Later, I learned that the Thuggee cult was once real, and did unspeakable things." He looked hard at Indiana. "I am ashamed of what happened here so many years ago. We keep these objects—these dolls and idols—to remind us that this will never again happen in my kingdom." His voice had risen by the end; a fine sweat lined his upper lip.

The room was hushed.

"Have I offended," Indiana finally said quietly. "Then I am sorry."

The room breathed again. Servants whisked away the old plates and brought in the new. Conversation resumed. Indy felt both more informed and more ignorant about the situation here.

"Ah," said the obese merchant beside Willie, "dessert!"

Short Round's monkey suddenly screeched and tore off through an open window. Willie closed her eyes: she would not look, it would be too gross, she didn't need this. She heard silverware clattering, though, and people digging in. Ultimately, curiosity prevailed, in conjunction with general lightheadedness; she opened her eyes.

It was instantly too late, though. She couldn't not see what she saw, and it was infinitely worse than she'd imagined.

Plates full of dead monkey heads.

The tops of the skulls had been cut off, and sat loose, like little lids, atop the scowling heads. Each plate sat on a small serving pedestal down which the long white monkey hair dangled from the little scalps.

Short Round looked shocked. Even Indy and Captain Blumburtt seemed somewhat unsettled, unsure.

Willie watched in utter dismay as the Maharajah and his guests removed the skull tops and began dipping small golden spoons into what was inside.

"Chilled monkey brains!" The merchant beside her could scarcely contain his delight.

Willie could scarcely contain anything else. So she dealt with the situation as honorably as she could, and fainted dead away.

"Rather bizarre menu, wouldn't you say?" Blumburtt remarked to Indiana as they strolled out of the pavilion, through the gardens. Short Round walked alongside. Hundreds of lanterns illuminated the after-dinner hour; the scent of the hookah mingled with the natural fragrances of the garden.

"Even if they were trying to scare us away, a devout Hindu would never touch meat," Indiana nodded. "Makes you wonder what these people are."

"Well," gruffed Blumburtt, "I hardly think they were trying to scare us."

Indy made a noncommittal expression. "Maybe not."

"Well, I must be off. Retire the troops and all that. Terribly nice to have met you, Doctor."

"Same here, Captain."

They shook hands once more; Blumburtt retreated.

Indy looked down at Shorty. "C'mon," he said. "Let's see what we can come up with."

They made their way around to the kitchen. Indy firmly believed that if you *really* wanted to learn something about a place, you talked to the servants.

A dozen people were back there cleaning up, washing dishes, putting things away. Indy spoke to the man who looked like the cook, but the man remained silent. Indy switched dialects. No response. He approached several others, all with the same results.

He saw a bowl of fruit on a sideboard, picked it up, asked if he could eat some. No one seemed to care.

"See, Shorty, it's just like I always say, you want to know about a household, you ask the help."

Short Round yawned.

Indy seconded the motion.

One young lady did look like she was winking at Indy—at least that's what he thought—but an older man immediately ushered her from the room. She left with a motion that Indy seconded even more heartily, a certain subtle motion of the hips that gave him a sudden wistful pang for a certain lady-in-waiting who was recently occupying a few of his thoughts.

He looked at the dour servants bustling about; he looked at the fruit bowl on the table; he looked at Shorty, dozing upright. He decided they *all* needed to relax a little.

Five minutes later, they were walking down the shadowy corridor to their bedroom. Short Round carried a covered plate, and yawned every ten seconds.

Indy patted him on the head, took the plate from him, stopped at their bedroom door. "Umm, I think I'd better check on Willie," he told the boy.

"That's all you better do," Shorty joked. He

backed into their room as Indy continued on down the hall; then whispered loudly: "Tell me later what happen."

Indy stopped short. "Amscray," he ordered. Shorty shut the door.

But he opened it a crack, just to watch, just for a minute. This was the beginning of the big love scene, after all, a union with potentially grave import for Short Round.

Just like the great Babe Ruth, Indy was about to score a home run—if he didn't strike out first.

Nothing would go wrong, though. Shorty was increasingly convinced that Indy and Willie were, in fact, the legendary lovers Hsienpo and Ying-t'ai, descended from the sky. Originally, they'd died in each other's arms, whereupon the Jade Emperor had sent them to live in all rainbows, Hsienpo being the red, Ying-t'ai the blue. And weren't Willie's eyes just that shade of blue? And didn't Indy's contain that reddish tinge? So now hadn't they obviously returned to join once more on earth and claim Short Round as the violet product of their fusion?

Short Round felt certain that they had.

For weren't his own brown eyes flecked with violet?

He could hardly keep his violet-flecked eyes open now, he was so sleepy. It made him wonder if Willie, like The Shadow, had the power to cloud men's minds. But Shorty would not sleep yet; he would at least witness the first coy twinings of this mythic pair.

Indy walked a few more steps to Willie's suite. The door was closed. He was about to knock, when it opened. Willie stood there, still in princess garb, looking mildly startled.

"My, what a surprise," she said.

"I've got something for you." Indy spoke from his throat. He was trying to be suave, though his face wasn't entirely in control.

"There's nothing you have that I could possibly want." She said it to tease, but even as she said it she knew she didn't really mean it.

"Right," nodded Indy. No point in sticking around where you weren't wanted. He turned to go, pulling an apple out from under the covered tray he carried. He bit down on it. Willie heard the crunch.

She grabbed the apple from him and took a bite. Apple never tasted so good. She closed her eyes, savoring the tart juices, the crisp texture. Heaven. As she opened her eyes, he took the cover off the tray, holding it up to her: bananas, oranges, pomegranates, figs, grapes.

Willie gasped. She took the tray into her room. He followed.

Short Round smiled wisely and went to bed.

Jones wasn't such a bad guy, really, Willie mused, if he were only a little less conceited. He *had* helped her out, though, and people *did* seem to have heard of him, so maybe he was actually sort of famous, and now this divine food, and you know, really he was very cute, and here they were thousands of miles from a radio or a car....

She stuffed a few more grapes in her mouth and smiled at him, standing there like a busboy in the doorway. *If driving fast cars you like, If low bars you like, If old hymns you like, If bare limbs you like* ... She rolled up her sleeves and peeled a banana. *If Mae West you like, Or me undressed you like, Why, nobody will oppose...*

He smiled back at her. The desperate girl. She obviously wanted him badly. Well, he didn't mind. She had what it took, and he certainly wouldn't refuse a little pick-me-up. He inched a step toward her.

"You're a nice man," she purred. "You could be my palace slave."

In fact, she'd been looking better each day. Gave him that old funny flutter to watch her now. "You wearing your jewels to bed, princess?"

"Yeah, and nothing else," she countered. "That shock you?" Anything goes.

"No." He moved up to her. "Nothing shocks me. I'm a scientist." He took the apple from her, chomped down on a mouthful.

"So," she said, "as a scientist, do you do a lot of research?"

"Always," he intimated.

"Oh, you mean like what kind of cream I put on my face at night, what position I like to sleep in, how I look in the morning?" This was getting kind of randy; she hoped he made his move soon.

Indy nodded as if he'd heard her thoughts. "Mating customs."

"Love rituals."

"Primitive sexual practices."

"So you're an authority in that area," she concluded, untying his tie. He was looking better all the time.

"Years of fieldwork," he admitted. Love in the tropics.

They kissed. Long, soft; controlled, but picking up speed.

They came up for air. "I don't blame you for being sore at me," she half-apologized. "I can be a real handful."

"I've had worse," he replied with *noblesse oblige*.

"You'll never have better," she promised.

"I don't know," he smirked, starting to close her door behind him. "As a scientist I hate to prejudice my experiment. I'll let you know in the morning."

Experiment! she thought, turning livid. *Like I'm his performing rat or something!* "What!" she hissed. She would be a lover, with pleasure; she would not be a conquest.

She opened the door he'd just shut. "Why, you conceited ape! I'm not that easy."

"Neither am I," he said, puzzled, then riled. "The trouble with you, Willie, is you're too used to getting your own way." He stalked out, to his own door across the hall.

"You're just too proud to admit you're crazy about me, Dr. Jones." *That* was *really* his problem: he had to be in control all the time, and being passionately in love with her made him feel too vulnerable, too much at her mercy. Well, she would show mercy— if he acted more like a gent.

"Willie, if you want me, you know where to find me." He stood in the doorway to his suite, trying to sound cool. She'd be around, soon enough.

"Five minutes," she predicted. "You'll be back here in five minutes." He wanted her more than he cared to admit; that was clear. He wouldn't last long in that state, poor boy.

Indy made a big show of yawning. "Sweetheart, I'll be *asleep* in five minutes." He closed the door.

"Five minutes," she repeated. "You know it, and I know it."

Indy opened his door a crack and peeped out, then closed it again. Willie slammed hers like the last word.

Indy stood in his room, leaning with his back against the door. No footfalls outside; no apologies forthcoming. Well, the hell with it. He walked over to his bed and sat down. Really steamed, and with good reason.

Willie marched away from her door, sat on the bed. She sank into the down mattress, muttering grimly. He'd be back. He wasn't all that smart, but he was a man—and she was a lot of woman. She picked up the clock by the bed and challenged it: "Five minutes." She took off her robe.

Indy took off his jacket. He glowered at the bedside clock. "Four and a half minutes," he grunted. Ridiculous. She was a ridiculous woman, this was a ridiculous palace, they were in a ridiculous situation, and he felt simply . . . put-upon.

Willie paced around her lavish suite. She blew out candles, turned down lamps, paused in front of the full-length mirror, began to primp. Her hair was really kind of a mess in all this dampness; could that have been the problem? She wished he hadn't stormed out *quite* so abruptly. But he'd be back.

Indy looked in his bureau mirror. So what was wrong with how he looked? Nothing, that's what. Of course she was a handsome woman, there was no denying that—but that was no reason to expect him to come groveling.

He walked over and tucked Shorty in on the couch. Ah, to be twelve again. Along the wall there were full-scale portraits of Rajput princes on prancing horses, palace landscapes, dancing girls. Dancing girls. Dancing girls.

Willie reclined on her four-poster bed, assuming various seductive poses. Periodically, she would look up, sweetly surprised at her contrite, imaginary visitor: "Why, Dr. Jones..." or, "Oh, Indiana..."

Her bedside clock said 10:18.

Indy lay on his bed, staring at the ceiling. How was he supposed to go to sleep now? Did she think he was made of steel? Could any man stand this kind of torture?

His bedside clock said 10:21.

Willie grabbed her clock, put it to her ear, shook it to see if it was working. Tick, tock, tick. She tapped her fingers irritably on the bedpost. Could her charms have failed? Was she losing her touch? How could he not be scratching at her door by now? How could he not?

Indy wanted to get up, but he refused to get up. The clock ticked beside him. He could wait her out; archaeology had trained him in the waiting game. Sooner or later she'd break down, give in, come around, hurry over. He just hoped it was sooner.

He looked toward the door. "Willie!" He smiled. The door remained closed. He tried a different voice. "Willie?" No. He tried nonchalance. "Willie. Oh, hi."

The door remained closed. Short Round kept sleeping.

In her room, Willie was trying new poses, new greetings. "Jones. Dr. Jones. Why, Indiana, hello."

Indiana's clock read 10:35. He smashed it to the floor and began to pace.

Willie slid to the foot of her bed, stretched out along the satin coverlet, arms akimbo. She slid off the end of the bed to the floor.

Indy paced back and forth along his row of wall

Indiana Jones, the
dashing archaeologist

Sassy nightclub singer,
Willie Scott

Short Round, Indy's
trusted sidekick

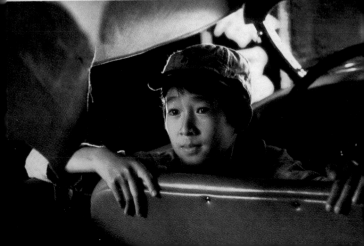

The Indian shaman greets our weary heroes

Listening to
the villagers'
story

En route to the Palace of Pankot

Indy examines the ancient inscriptions

The deadly spikes get closer and closer

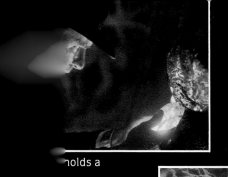

...holds a

...dy is captured...

Willie is to be
...ext sacrifice!

Short Round
escapes

Indy frees
the children

The only way out!

Trapped!

Indy hangs on as
the guards fall
around him

Indy, Willie and Short Round return to the village in triumph

paintings of princes, prancing horses, and dancing girls, and dancing girls.

Willie paced back and forth along her row of wall paintings, muttering. "Nocturnal activities, crap! Primitive sexual practices! 'I'll tell you in the morning.'"

Indy began muttering too, in his truncated promenade. "Palace slave. I'm a conceited ape. Five minutes."

Willie stopped pacing. She stared at herself in the mirror, dumbfounded, frustrated, bewildered. "I can't believe it: he's not coming."

Indy stopped pacing, stared into space. "I can't believe it: she's not coming. I can't believe it: I'm not going."

From behind the last wall painting stepped a darkly clothed guard, who slipped a strangling cord around Indiana's neck.

Jones managed to get a few fingers around the garrote, but even so, he could feel his larynx nearly crushed within a matter of seconds. Gasping futilely for air, he sank slowly to his knees. His eyes bulged as he stared at the tiny, smiling skulls on the ends of the death-cord clutched in the assassin's fists. With a last, lunging effort, Indiana bent forward sharply: the guard spilled over his back onto the floor.

The guard pulled a knife, but Indiana smashed him in the head with a pot; the dagger clattered to the ground. Short Round began to stir. Indy heard something in the hall and looked up at the door. The guard jumped him again.

In the hall, Willie stood shouting at Indiana's closed door. "This is one night you'll never forget! It's the night I slipped right through your fingers!

Sleep tight, Dr. Jones. Pleasant dreams. I could've been your greatest adventure."

Indy flipped back over the guard; the two of them tumbled across the tiles. Short Round woke up with a start. As Indy stood shakily, Shorty grabbed the whip, tossed it over. Indy caught it.

He whipped the assassin's arm, but the man unleashed himself and ran toward the door. Indy lashed out again, this time catching the guard around the neck. The thug yanked on it; the handle flew out of Indy's hand, up to the ceiling fan.

The whip twisted around the revolving blades like fishing line around a reel. And like a doomed flounder, the assassin was slowly dragged toward the ceiling. His toes lifted off the marble floor. He let out a short, choked scream.... His legs twitched... and he was hanged.

"Shorty, turn off the fan!" Indy shouted. "I'm gonna check Willie."

Shorty hit the wall switch; the fan stopped as Indy ran from the room.

He burst into Willie's suite, wild-eyed.

She lay on the bed, heart a-flutter. "Oh, Indy." He'd come after all. Sweet man. Maybe he just didn't know how to tell time.

He dove onto the bed.

"Be gentle with me," she whispered.

He scrambled across the bed, looked underneath it. Empty. He got up and began a furious search of the room.

"I'm *here*," Willie called.

Indy continued his frantic examination. Willie drew aside the bed curtains. His eyes had doubtless misted with love: he wasn't seeing clearly.

Indy walked around the end of the bed, stood in front of the doors. "Nobody here," he muttered.

"No, I'm here," cooed Willie, drawing the last curtain.

Indy moved over to the mirror. Willie jumped off the bed and followed him. He felt a draft by the vase of flowers, coming from somewhere over to the left. The assassin had entered through a secret passage in his room; there had to be one in this chamber as well.

He walked over to a pillar. The draft was stronger here.

Willie still followed him. "Indy, you're acting awfully strange."

Indy looked at the pillar: a naked dancing-girl was carved into the stone. He began feeling around the carving's protuberances: shoes, baubles, hips, breasts.

Willie thought this was *exceedingly* strange. "Hey, I'm right *here*."

The lever was in the breasts. Suddenly the entire pillar disappeared into the wall with a grinding creak, forming an entranceway into a tunnel.

Indy walked in. He struck a match, read the inscription on the wall: "'Follow in the footsteps of Shiva.'"

"What does that mean?" whispered Willie excitedly. She was right behind him now.

"'Do not betray...'" He stopped, removed the small fragment of ancient cloth from his pocket, compared it with the inscription on the wall.

Shorty appeared in the doorway now, and approached the niche.

Indy read the Sanskrit on the piece of cloth. "'Do

not betray his truth.'" He turned to the boy. "Shorty, get our stuff."

Short Round ran back to the bedroom as Indy turned into the tunnel.

6

The Temple of Doom

"What's down there?" quaked Willie.

"That's what I'm going to find out. You wait here. If we're not back in an hour, I want you to wake Captain Blumburtt and come after us."

She nodded. Short Round returned with Indy's bag, whip, and hat, and the two of them started down the secret passage.

Shorty led the way around the first corner, to make sure it was safe for Indy. The shadows looked pretty ominous, though. "Dr. Jones, I don't think we supposed to be here."

Indy grabbed him by the collar, planted him to the rear. "Stay behind me, Short Round. Step where I step. And don't touch anything."

As Indy moved forward, however, Short Round noticed a door off to the side, a door Indy had missed. Short Round put his hand on the knob and pulled:

the door collapsed: two skeletons fell forward on top of him.

Shorty yelled, sitting down hard. He'd seen these guys before—in *The Mummy*. He thought he'd made it quite clear then, to Whoever was in charge, that he never wanted to run into anyone in this condition, especially not in a dark tunnel. Someone must be trying to teach him a lesson.

Indy pulled him erect, half-carried him around the next turn. A hollow wind sprang up here, blowing flayed skins in their faces—human skins, they looked like.

Short Round drew his knife. "I step where you step. I touch nothing."

More skins flapped in their faces. Shorty broke into a voluble string of Chinese prayers, epithets, and warnings about ghosts. More like *The Invisible Man*, here: tattered coverings falling away from an empty presence. Shorty was glad he'd seen such creatures before, so he wouldn't be undone now.

"Relax, kid." Indy smiled grimly. "They're just trying to scare us."

They kept walking. The tunnel was stone—cool, moist, solid. The farther they went, the more it seemed to twist downwards into the earth, and the darker it got.

Soon it became too black to see.

"All right, it all gets dark now," said Indy. "Stick close."

A few more paces, and Shorty felt something crunchy underfoot. "I step on something," he whispered.

"Yeah, there's something on the ground."

"Feel like I step on fortune cookies."

"Not fortune cookies." Indy shook his head. It

was moving, whatever it was. He struck a match; they looked around. Before them was a wall with two holes in it. Out of one of the holes exuded an effluent of gooey mung, and millions of squirming, wriggling bugs. The bugs poured out onto the floor, covering it completely: a living carpet of shiny beetles, scurrying roaches, wriggling larvae.

Short Round looked down to see a few of them start to crawl up his leg. "That no cookie." He winced.

Indy brushed the bugs off. At the same moment, the match he was holding burned down to his fingertip and went out. "Ow! Go!" he shouted, pushing his small friend ahead of him. They ran quickly, dashing directly into the next chamber.

Just past the threshold, Shorty stepped on a small button in the floor. This triggered the mechanism that started a great stone door rolling shut behind them.

"Oh, no," breathed Indy. He dove back, tried to hold it open.

But it closed.

As he turned, he saw the door on the opposite side of the cave slide down: the dim light emanating from beyond it was extinguished. Indy dove toward the portal—but again, he was too late.

He sat on the floor a moment, collecting his thoughts.

"Are you mad at me?" Shorty asked in a small voice out of the darkness. He felt like one of the Little Thunders—children of My Lord the Thunder and the Mother of Lightnings, who, through well-intentioned in experience, were always having misadventures.

"Indy, you mad at me?"

"No," Indiana mumbled. And then, more softly: "Not exactly." Mad at *himself* was more like it. He never should have brought the kid down here; it was too dangerous.

"Oh, you just angry?"

"Right," said Indy, striking a match. He found a piece of oily rag on the floor and lit it. Human skeletons littered the ground. Shorty moved toward him. Indiana didn't want the boy inadvertently stumbling into any other trigger mechanisms, though. "Stop right there," he warned Shorty. "Look, go stand up against the wall."

Short Round did as he was told. He flattened his back against a block protruding from the stone wall. The block slid into the wall, triggering another device.

From the ceiling, spikes began to lower.

"Oh, no," groaned Indiana.

The burning rag illuminated the spikes as if they were the fiery teeth of hell.

Short Round shouted angrily at Indy, "You say stand against wall, I listen to what you say. Not my fault, not my fault!"

Indy wasn't listening, though. He was shouting through the door at the top of his voice. "Willie, get down here!"

Back in her room, Willie heard Indy call. She pulled on her robe, stepped into the drafty tunnel. "Indy!" she yelled back. There was no answer. She grabbed a small oil lamp from the table, began walking down the corridor. "I bet I get all dirty again," she muttered, rounding the first turn.

The two skeletons leapt out at her. "Indy!" she screamed. "There's two dead people in here!"

"There's going to be two dead people in *here* if you don't hurry up!" he shouted back.

She ran past the disgusting, flapping skins, down the steep grade, into the deepening dark, the rising wind. The wind blew out her lamp. Then came the foul odor.

"Ooh, it stinks in here," she moaned.

"Willie, get down here!"

"I've had almost enough of you two," she barked. What did they think, she did this for a living?

"Willie!"

The ceiling spikes were coming lower, getting closer. They looked more like sword blades now, with razor cutting edges.

"I'm coming," she hollered.

"C'mon, we're in trouble!" he roared. Then to Short Round: "Give me your knife." He took the dagger from Shorty, began digging frantically at the inset block of stone.

"What sort of trouble?" she called.

Spikes were rising from the floor now as well. "Deep trouble."

"Indy?" She kept walking. The smell got worse as his voice got louder.

"This is serious," he urged her on.

"What's the rush?"

"It's a long story. Hurry or you won't get to hear it."

"Oh, God, what is this?" She stopped at the new sensation underfoot. "There's stuff all over the floor. It's kind of crispy...and then it goes kind of creamy. Indy, what is it? I can't see a thing."

She struck a match.

All over: bugs.

Skittering beetles with black carapaces, long-legged arthropods, puffy translucent things that resembled scorpions, squirming wormy things, hopping locusts, segmented cave things...

It made her too sick to scream; all she could do was gag. "Indy, let me in. There's bugs all over here, Indy."

"Willie," Indy explained to her from the other side of the stone door that separated them, "there are no bugs in here."

"Open the door and let me in," she begged.

"Open the door and let us out," wailed Shorty. "Let us out, let us out!"

"Let me in, Indy, please," she squeaked.

"Right. Workin' on it."

"Indy, they're in my hair." Making nests there, burrowing in, spinning webs, clicking their pincers.

"Willie, shut up and listen. There's got to be a fulcrum release lever."

"A what?"

"A handle that opens the door."

"Oh, God, Indy. They're in my hair." Scratching, nibbling.

The tips of the spikes were now at head level.

"Open your eyes, Willie. Look around. There's got to be a lever hidden somewhere. Go on, look."

"There's two holes," she whimpered. "I see two square holes."

"Right. Now go to the right hole."

Sure. The one with all the mung and bugs oozing out of it. This was a joke, right?

Tentatively, she stretched her hand toward the left-sided hole, the relatively clean one. Not clean, exactly, of course, but at least not that disgusting slime-infested...

A hand reached through the left hole and grabbed hers. Indy's hand.

"No, not that hole, the other one!" he shouted. "The hole on your right!"

"It looks alive inside. I can't do it," she protested.

"You can do it. Feel inside," he guided her. Come on, kiddo, I need your help.

"*You* feel inside." Big wheel, telling her what to do.

"You've got to do it now!" he yelled. He was scrunched way down already; the spikes were pressing his flesh.

Willie eased her hand into the mess. "Oh, God, it's soft. It's moving. It's like a bowl of rotten peaches."

"Willie, we are going to die."

"I got it." She found a lever and yanked. The door rolled back.

Indy sat there beside Shorty, inside the doorway, as the spikes slowly started to recede.

Willie ran in tearing the bugs from her hair, shivering at the feel of their little feet all over her skin.

Shorty ran to the opposite door, which was sliding up, and took a long slide across the threshold— just like the immortal Ty Cobb stealing second. He wanted out of there, before anything else went wrong.

Willie stomped and shook. "Get them off me. They're all over me, get them off, I hate bugs, they're in my hair."

As she bent down to comb them out, she pushed in the block that was the trigger mechanism for the whole thing to start over again.

The first door commenced to roll shut.

Short Round called from the opposite door: "I didn't do it. She did it. Come on, get out!"

He began burbling in his native language as the far door, and the spikes, began once more descending. Like a Cantonese Little League third-base coach, he shouted in Chinese: "Slide, Indy, slide!"

Indy took hold of Willie; they sprinted across the room. He pushed her under the falling door, then dove under himself, just knocking his hat off on the way out.

And then, with inches to spare, he reached back in under the descending door, grabbed his hat, and pulled it out moments before the door crashed into place.

You should never go on an adventure without your hat.

They found themselves in a large, eerily lit tunnel through which blew a strange and forlorn wind, howling like a dirge from the earth's own core.

The light came from up ahead, around a curve in the tunnel. Reddish light; brooding, spectral. Indy, Willie, and Short Round walked slowly to the mouth of the tunnel; then stared, astonished, at the sight below them.

It was a cavern, staggeringly vast, carved over every inch of its surface, as if it had been carved out of the solid mass of the rock, carved with a vaulted, cathedrallike ceiling supported by rows of stone columns, carved into a colossal, subterranean temple. A temple of death.

Stone balconies overhung the granite floor, supported by pillars and arches that led off to dark side chambers. From these grottos poured worshippers, hundreds of them, chanting as they entered the temple. They chanted in unison, in response to the bizarre, lonely winds that howled out of the tunnels that pierced the upper levels of the cavern.

This strange tunnel-music created its own harmonics, its own dynamics, rising and falling in pitch and volume, echoing off all of the resonant hollows. And as these winds galed or died, the worshippers droned in answer, loud, or discordant, or muted, or keening: "Gho-ram gho-ram gho-ram sundaram, gho-ram gho-ram gho-ram sunda-ram..."

Mammoth stone statues loomed around the swelling congregation, rock, fashioned into elephants, lions, demigods and demons; ornate monstrosities, half-human, half-animal, some surely erupted from the mind of madness.

Torches were lit over the balconies, affording a clearer view to the three onlookers who stared, transfixed, from their tiny perch high above and to the rear of the scene. Below them, the mystery cult began bowing toward an enormous altar at the far end of the temple. Separating them from this altar was a crevasse—it looked partly natural, partly carved and shaped—from which the dull red light emanated, out of which sulfurous wisps of smoke and steam rose until they were sucked away up some nether tunnel by the moaning, baying winds.

The altar itself, on the far side of the crevasse, was roiled in smoke, obscuring its precise shape. As the ceremony continued, robed priests emerged from this miasma, carrying pots of incense, clearing the air around the altar as they came forward to the far edge of the crevasse. Soon, the incense dissipated; a giant stone statue appeared on the altar, its back to the far wall, standing partly within an enormous, domed niche carved into the stuff of the rock.

It was Kali—the hideous protectress of the temple, the malevolent, bloodthirsty goddess who was the object of all this devotion.

She stood twenty feet tall. Carved snakes curled up her legs, while girdling her hips was a skirt of hanging human arms. The statue itself had six arms: one held a saber; one grasped the severed head of a giant victim by the hair; two supported her on the altar; two, outstretched, dangled a flat, iron-mesh basket on chains.

Around her shoulders were draped necklaces of human skulls.

Her face was vile, half mask, half ghoul: a loathesome miscreant. Her eyes and mouth glowed with molten lava from the pit below, scorching her stony fangs black; there was no nose, only a deformed hole; her headdress was carved with ancient markings that bespoke great evil.

The priests gazed up at the deity reverently. The worshippers chanted louder, in a growing passion of foul cravings.

Up in the wind tunnel, Willie shivered. "What's happening?" she whispered. It made her feel cold, hollow; shaken.

"It's a Thuggee ceremony," said Indy. "They're worshipping Kali."

"Ever seen this before?"

"Nobody's seen this for over a hundred years." He was excited, on edge. What an incredible discovery he'd stumbled upon! An extinct religion, its rituals and totems as alive now as they'd ever been. It was as if he were viewing the reanimated bones of a lost tribe.

Suddenly they heard a wailing from behind the altar—inhuman, but all too human.

"Baachao; muze baachao. Baachao koi muze-baachao."

"What's that?" muttered Willie.

"Sounds like the main event," Indy replied. "He's calling 'Save me, someone please save me.'"

Grimly they watched as the ritual continued.

A huge drum sounded three times; the chanting stopped. Only the wind sustained a relentless groan. In the chill of its echo, another figure stepped forward onto the altar. This was the High Priest, Mola Ram.

His robes were black, his eyes red and sunken. He wore a necklace of teeth. On his head sat the upper skull of a bison, its horns curling out like those of the devil incarnate.

He walked to the edge of the crevasse, facing the crowd. Just the other side of the pit, facing the High Priest, Indy noticed a familiar figure sitting. "Look," he said quietly to Willie. "Our host, the Maharajah."

"Who's the guy he's lookin' at?" Willie nodded.

"Looks like the High Priest."

To Short Round, he looked like Frankenstein.

Mola Ram lifted his arms above his head. Again, a pitiful scream rose from behind the altar, as if it were coming from the statue of Kali herself. Quickly the true sound of the scream became identifiable: a struggling, ragged Indian was dragged out onto the altar by priests and tied to the rectangular iron frame basket that hung from Kali's arms, just above the stone floor.

All watched in silence.

Mola Ram walked over to the bound victim, who was writhing helplessly, spread-eagled on his back atop the hanging frame. The man wailed. Mola Ram uttered an incantation. The man sobbed. Mola Ram extended his hand towards the bound man; his hand pierced the victim's chest.

Pierced it, sank into the poor, squirming torso... and ripped out the Indian's living heart.

Willie covered her mouth.

Short Round's eyes opened wide. "He pulled his heart out. He's dead." Emperor Shou-sin used to remove the hearts of sages, Short Round had heard, to see if it was true that the heart of a sage is pierced with seven holes. This man's heart had no holes, though, and that priest wasn't Shou-sin. To Short Round, it looked like they'd fallen into hell.

There were ten hells, ruled by the Yama Kings. At various levels, a person might be buried in a lake of ice, bound to a red-hot pillar, drowned in a pool of fetid blood, reincarnated as a Famished Demon; many tortures were there.

This was certainly the fifth hell, in which the dead soul's heart was repeatedly plucked out.

Short Round did not want to be here.

Indy didn't believe in hell. But he believed in what he saw. And what he saw now was more un-believable than any hell he'd ever imagined. He stared, rapt, at the man being sacrificed.

"He's still alive," murmured Indiana.

Indeed, the man still screamed, and his bloody heart maintained a steady beat in Mola Ram's hand. Mola Ram lifted the heart above his head. Once again, the worshippers began to chant:

"Jai ma Kali, jai ma Kali, jai ma Kali..."

The sacrificial victim kept wailing, very much alive. There was no evidence of a gash on his chest, only a reddish mark where Mola Ram's hand had entered.

The priests added chains to the iron frame, up-ended it, then reversed its orientation so that the man was suspended face-down, suspended above a massive stone door in the floor—a door that began rolling away with a sonorous rumble, to reveal the same pit below him as the one at the bottom of the crevasse: bubbling, crimson lava.

And then the iron frame was lowered into the pit.

The victim saw the fiery magma slowly rise to meet him. His heart continued to beat in Mola Ram's hand. The crowd kept chanting, the wind continued to howl: these were the last sounds he heard on this earth.

His face began to smoke and blister as the lava flared closer to his lowering body. His flesh sizzled, peeled, charred. He tried to scream, but the noxious fumes filled his lungs; the superheated vapors seared his throat.

His hair burst into flame.

Finally, the frame submerged into the boiling, molten ore.

Up in the tunnel, Willie closed her eyes; Indy watched in horror; Short Round looked, and turned away, and looked again. He appealed to the Celestial Ministry of Fire to deliver them from this hellish domain.

Beside the altar, Mola Ram held the heart high: still beating, dripping blood, it began to smoke. Then it, too, burst into flame. And then it disappeared.

The iron frame was raised, on its winches, out of the chasm by priests who turned a great wheel at the side of the altar. The metal glowed red, like a brand, but there was no trace of the sacrificed victim. He'd been completely incinerated.

The multitudes chanted. "Jai ma Kali, Jai ma Kali, gho-ram, sundaram..."

The wind railed.

Indy, Willie, and Short Round stared, glassy-eyed, at this thing they'd just witnessed.

Mola Ram left, behind the altar. Three priests emerged from the shadows, carrying cloth-wrapped objects toward the altar.

Willie began to cry.

"Quiet," whispered Indy; but Short Round looked on the verge himself, and hugged Willie close.

The priests carefully unwrapped three conical pieces of crystallized quartz, bringing these tokens to the base of the statue of Kali. Mounted between the statue's legs was a four-foot-tall stone skull, its eyes and nose hollow. The priests brought the three crystals together in front of the skull. The stones began to glow with a burning, incandescent radiance. The priests pulled the stones apart; the glowing stopped. They brought them together once more, nestling them in the three waiting skull sockets. The stones glowed brightly.

Indiana watched in mounting fascination. "They knew their rock was magic. But they didn't know it was one of the lost Sankara Stones."

"Why does it glow in the dark?" Short Round trembled.

"Legend says that when the stones are brought together, the diamonds inside them will glow."

Willie wiped her eyes, pulled herself together. She almost laughed, from fatigue and tension. "Diamonds?" She nudged him with renewed interest.

The Sankara Stones shimmered brilliantly, seducing all caught in the web of their luminescent power. The three bearer priests bowed repeatedly to the crystals, finally backing out on their knees, into the dark space behind the altar.

The other priests followed. Then the entire crowd started dispersing. In a couple of minutes, the cavern was empty once more. Only the wind cried at the horror.

Indiana turned to his friends. "All right, now listen: you two wait here and keep quiet."

Short Round nodded. He was in no hurry to go any closer. He handed Indy the bullwhip and shoulder bag. Willie didn't look so sure.

"Wait. What're you doing?" she demanded. She just wanted to get out of here.

Indy peered down the sheer drop from the mouth of the wind tunnel to the stone floor far below. "Going down there," he advised her.

"Down there? Are you crazy?"

"I'm not leaving without those stones." They were the find of the century; they'd touched him with their glow; he had to have them.

She was suddenly furious. "You're gonna get killed chasing after your damn fortune and glory!"

He looked at her with real warmth in this dank place: she cared for what happened to him. "Maybe, someday," he smiled affectionately. "Not today." Today, he was going to own those magic stones.

Without waiting for her reply, he lowered himself meticulously out the mouth of the tunnel.

There were plenty of footholds and handholds in the pocked stone. With skill, Indy was able to maneuver himself over and down to one of the monumental supporting columns near the rear of the cavern. Once there, he inched down the pillar, hanging on to stone cobras, sculpted lions, carved dancing maidens. After what seemed a long time, he made it all the way to the bottom.

Quietly he ran across the length of the chamber, stopping when he came to the crevasse. He looked down. Fire bubbled there, like the liquid soul of the temple. Its fumes stung his eyes and nostrils; he had to step back.

Across the gulf stood the statue of Kali, and, before her, the three Sankara Stones. It was too wide to jump across. Indiana looked from side to side; no way around, either.

Then he noticed two columns on the far side of the abyss, on top of which stone elephants perched, flanking the altar. Indy uncurled his whip and, with master precision, let it fly.

The bullwhip cracked. Its end wrapped tightly around the tusk of the closer stone elephant. Indy tugged on the whip handle, pulled the thong taut, took a deep breath . . . and ran.

At the edge, he leaped. The whip snapped tight as he cleared the lip. Then he was arching down, then up, across the fiery breach.

He landed on his feet, near the towering goddess. The wind rose, in a mocking warble. Indy released the whip end from the elephant's tusk.

Short Round waved to him from the elevated wind tunnel: all clear. It was hard being a bodyguard long-distance, but Shorty took the job seriously even at the outposts. Indy nodded, re-coiling the whip onto his belt. He turned toward the altar. There the three stones continued to glow. Cautiously, Indiana approached.

He stooped to examine them closely. The middle

stone—the one stolen from Mayapore village—had three lines painted across it. They glimmered intensely. Indy touched it: it didn't burn. Carefully, he lifted it to his face, peered into its glowing matter.

A magical diamond sparkled within the substance of the rock. Its light was ethereal, hypnotic. Beautiful. Rainbow light. Star light. But as soon as it was away from its niche a few moments, its light dwindled and died. Indy brought it near the other two again; again, they all glowed intensely. Apart, dark; together, bright.

He put the jewels in his pouch.

All of them touching, in the sack—it was like a tiny, cool sun.

Willie and Short Round apprehensively watched Indy bag the three Sankara Stones. He pulled the drawstrings tight, sealing off the emanation.

Kali, too, watched.

Indiana backed off, looked up at the horrific statue. Kali looked down on the puny mortal...and spoke.

Indiana jumped back. The demonic face seemed to laugh at him, to echo, to mumble, accuse...

Wait. The sounds were coming from behind the altar, not from the mouth of the statue. Indy chuckled at himself—though not too loudly—and walked around behind the altar to see what the noises were.

Willie and Short Round grew immediately concerned as Indy disappeared from sight beyond the altar.

"Oh, hell, *now* where's he going?" she whispered harshly. She did not like being left alone.

The wind was moaning again. The note in their tunnel began to quaver slightly, though, to shift its pitch in a series of funny staccato modulations. Short Round turned to see two shadowy figures moving down the tunnel toward him: their bodies moving through the wind tunnel altered the tone, creating the eerie harmonics.

Short Round froze.

"What're you—" Willie began—but then she saw.

In another second the two huge Thuggee guards were lunging at them. Short Round drew his dagger in time to slash the closer Thug's hand. The man fell back, in surprise and pain. The other guard grabbed Willie.

She'd been wrestling with goons like this one for as long as she'd worn lipstick, though. With a well-practiced move, she brought her knee up sharply into his groin. He groaned, and sank to his haunches.

The other guard was now cautiously closing in on Short Round. Willie jumped up on the lug's back, wrapping her hands around his face, going for the eyes. He swung around, slamming her into the wall. She slumped to the ground, the wind knocked out of her. In that moment Shorty stuck the guard in the leg, then backed off again. He and the wounded guard circled.

The other Thug started crawling toward Willie. When he was a few feet away, she scooped up a big handful of dirt and hurled it into his face. The man clawed blindly at his eyes as Willie stood up.

"Run, Willie! Run!" Short Round called. He still kept the other guard at bay: like Dizzy Dean, holding the runner at first.

Willie ran ten yards up the tunnel, then stopped and turned. Shorty swung his dagger in tight arcs, keeping his distance from the assassin. Suddenly the guard shouted something in Hindi, and dove,

130

knocking Short Round off his feet. The knife clattered to the dirt. He grabbed Shorty by the ankle, and dragged the boy, kicking, to him.

Willie hesitated. The other guard was stumbling to his feet. This wasn't working.

"Run!" screamed Short Round. "Go get help!"

Willie ran back up the tunnel. The last thing she saw was Short Round being lifted bodily by the throat, until his little feet dangled helplessly above the ground.

Meanwhile, Indiana entered the darkened chamber behind the altar. The only illumination came from two places: the smoky red light from the inferno in the temple, streaming in here around the gigantic silhouetted statue of Kali; and, up ahead, a dim cylindrical shaft of yellowish light rising from what appeared to be an enormous hole in the ground.

Indy slowly crossed a narrow stone bridge toward the hole—a bridge over what, it was too dark to tell. Presently he reached the other side, though. As he neared the great cavity, he began to hear voices, and the clink of metal against rock. The ground was inordinately dark; he crept toward the precipice with extreme uncertainty, ready to run on short notice. He reached the edge, and looked down.

What he saw was a wide, deep pit, around the sides of which concentric paths spiraled leading off into numerous narrow tunnels. Crawling in and out of the burrows, scrawny children lugged sacks of dirt and rock. Other hollow-eyed kids, mostly chained, pulled these sacks to mine cars parked on rails that crisscrossed the excavation.

It was a mine.

Torchlight cast weird dancing shadows across the walls. Beyond the farthest tracks in the main excavation site, a vertical stream of water hugged the cavern wall, filling a massive cistern that overflowed into a sparkling dark pool. Machines whined; exhaust fumes hung in the stagnant air; black fires erupted from vents in the rock; sparks billowed out of holes where iron grated on stone.

Children were whimpering or silent, according to inclination; none were other than miserable, though. Sadistic Thuggee guards lashed at them, or beat them mercilessly. Some laughed.

Indy saw several children slip and fall while straining to lift a bag of rocks into one of the mine cars. Guards kicked them. One child didn't get up; fortunate soul, he had finally found his only escape from this travail in hell.

Indiana edged around the pit. It was ghastly, a scene so grotesque as to defy comprehension. He couldn't fathom what to do. This was beyond anything involved with even the most ghoulish rites of the most pagan religion.

He hefted the bag of stones on his shoulder. They burdened him now with choices: he could leave, if he wanted, with the Sankara Stones in his possession, priceless artifacts to be studied and prized for centuries yet to come.

But he could hear the pleading of a child. He looked down to see a huge, burly, bare-chested guard cruelly beating the pitiful little slave. The fury welled up in Indiana without release. He clenched his fists; he ground his teeth.

The guard seemed to feel the intense pressure of Indy's stare on his back. He stopped beating the child; looked up at Indy looking down. Their gazes met, locked, wrestled. Slackly, the guard smiled: he was enjoying himself.

The brute was far below him. Indy could still leave, if he chose.

His choice wasn't hard.

He bent down, picked up a rock, stood, held it over his head, took aim, and flung it down into the mine.

By the time it hit bottom, it must have been going at a pretty good clip, but the guard just caught it. Just plain caught it. It bent him over some; then he straightened up, looked back at Indy. Their eyes met again; again the guard smiled—only this time he was memorizing Indy's face: imprinting every last detail on his brain, so he would not forget this puny insurgent who had dared annoy him.

Indy returned the smile, though he knew this wasn't a real good first round. The startled slave children looked up at him in shock. He postured victoriously and doffed his hat at the bewildered Thuggee guards who ran over to see what the commotion was.

This is just the beginning, you bastards, he thought. He began to look for a boulder, when something unnerving happened: dirt started crumbling away from the rim of the pit. A small landslide, in fact.

And then, as luck would have it, a big landslide.

In the space of a backstep, the entire floor gave way; that section of the rim sheared off, and Indy toppled with it. Debris and Indiana went plunging into the mine, bouncing off dirt ledges and loose clay, until he lay in a pile of rubble at the bottom of the shaft.

Bruised and cut, he looked up. Thuggee guards

surrounded him, appearing much larger and angrier than they had just a few moments before.

He smiled at the big one, shaking his head. "How did you get so ugly?"

7

. . . And into the Fire

The guards grabbed him, clubbed him, dragged him into a small holding cell. There they chained his wrists to the low roof. The pain of the manacles cutting into his arms woke him in time to see the barred door slam shut. As it was being padlocked, three other prisoners who'd been cowering in the corner of the cell ran up to him. Two of them were Indian slave children; one was Short Round.

Tearfully the boy hugged Indy. Shackled as he was, Indiana could not return the embrace. Below them, in the quarry, he heard children being whipped. It was the foulest sound he'd ever heard. He had to get out of here.

Shorty stepped back and began scolding him. "You promise to take me to America. This doesn't happen in America. I keep telling you: you listen to me more, you live longer." It was outrageous! Indy, caught like a Little Thunder.

Indy nodded, smiling. He wondered if Shorty could talk him out of his irons. If Willie were here, she could for sure.

Short Round pointed to one of the boys beside him. "This is Nainsukh, from that village. He speak pretty good English for a foreigner. He say they bring him here to dig in the mines."

"But why?" Indy asked.

"Children are small," said Nainsukh. "We can work in tunnels."

"Why are you two locked up, then?"

"Now we are too old—too big to crawl into the little tunnels—" The boy's throat choked with emotion; he had to stop speaking.

"What they do to you now?" Short Round asked, his pupils dilated in fear of the answer.

"I pray to Shiva to let me die," wavered Nainsukh, "but I do not. Now the evil of Kali will take me."

"How?"

"They will make me drink the blood of Kali. Then I fall into black sleep of Kali Ma."

"What's that?" Indy stopped him.

The boy steeled himself against the vision of what he was going to be forced to do. "We become like them. We be alive, but like in nightmare. You drink the blood, you not wake up from nightmare of Kali Ma."

Indy and Short Round saw the terror on the child's face. Shorty fervently spoke the name of the God of the Door of Ghosts. Indy vowed revenge, in the name of these nameless children. Suddenly there was a clanking noise. Indy saw two guards unlocking the door to the cell.

Nainsukh and the other boy yelped, ran to the

back of their cage, trembled in the darkness like trapped animals awaiting the inevitable.

The guards weren't there for the children, though; they were there for Indy and Short Round. They unchained Indiana, marched the two friends out of the cell, up the winding path that curved around the sides of the mine pit, down a long dark tunnel. At the end of the tunnel, a thick wooden door opened. The prisoners were shoved inside.

They stumbled into the chamber. It was the chamber of the High Priest, Mola Ram.

The place was a gallery of terror. Ritualistic statues and grisly icons covered the walls, staring down like all the eyes of Evil. The rock itself seemed somehow deformed. Small fissures perforated the floor, leaking red steam, filling the cave with a putrid essence. It made Indy want to choke.

In one corner, an iron pot was filled to overflowing with burning coals and strange incense. It was tended by an androgynous man with painted lips, thin arms, delicate hands, a face rank with madness. He stirred the coals, humming a twilight melody.

Across the room stood the most grotesque statue Indiana had ever seen. It could only have been nightmare-spawned; it was the stone effigy of Death.

Twice human size, its head was formed into the shape of a skull—but a skull too big in back, as if malformed, or hydrocephalic, with its jawbone dangling open too wide, in a demented grimace. A candle burned in each eyesocket, and atop its forehead.

Its body was no skeleton body, however. It was a woman's body, but also mutant: no neck, no arms, asymmetric breasts, legs that fused into a morbid, lumpy base.

Candlewax ran down its stone head, out of its

eyes into its nasal cavity, down its hanging jaw, like drool, over its stumpy shoulders, down its swollen breasts—candlewax, and, Indy could see now, just beginning to congeal: fresh blood.

Beside the foul thing stood a giant, bearded Thuggee guard, grinning insanely, wearing bracelets of human hair. It was the same guard Indy had thrown the rock at, the one who'd caught it. Now he'd caught Indy; now he was going to get even.

And in the center of the room, crosslegged, his eyes closed, sat Mola Ram.

This was the first opportunity Indy had to see him up close. He was a loathesome sight. His bison-skull headdress cradled his brow; affixed to its center was a shrunken human head. His face was hideously painted in some occult design. His teeth were bad; his eyes were sunken. His sweat smelled of rotting flesh.

His eyes opened; he smiled. "I am Mola Ram. You were caught trying to steal the Sankara Stones."

"Nobody's perfect." Indy smiled in return.

The stones began to glow. He hadn't seen them before, but there they were, near the base of the statue—glowing, seemingly in response to the High Priest's state of agitation.

Mola Ram's eyes glazed over as he stared, absorbed, at the pulsing crystals. "There were five stones in the beginning," he said. "Over the centuries they were dispersed by wars, sold off by thieves like you."

"Better thieves than me," Indiana said modestly. "You're still missing two."

"No, they are here," Mola Ram protested. "Somewhere, they are here. A century ago, when the British raided this temple and butchered my people," he decried, "a loyal priest hid the last two stones down here in the catacombs."

Suddenly Indy realized what this treachery was all about. "That's what you've got these slaves digging for, these children." The anger started to churn within him again.

"They dig for gems to support our cause," Mola Ram assented, "and yes, they also search for the last two stones. Soon we will have all five Sankara Stones, and then the Thuggee will be all-powerful."

"Can't accuse you of having a vivid imagination," Indiana jibed.

"You do not believe me." The High Priest focused on Indy now. "You will, Dr. Jones. You will become a *true* believer."

He gave a sign. The guards clamped an iron collar around Indiana's neck, dragged him over to the Death statue, and chained him to it, his back pressing into its front, the chains stretching from his neck and wrists around behind the idol's backside. He could smell the blood that stained its chin.

He was afraid. This fevered air, these maniac priests—anything could happen. He wouldn't show his fear, though; he wouldn't give them the satisfaction. These fanatics thrived on fear, fear and suffering. He would not sate their lusts. And he would not give Short Round cause to despair, for the boy still stood, trembling, near the front of the room. He would set an example for Short Round, show him dignity could rise above defilement, even in a place as degraded as this...if you were strong of heart.

The giant guard strode forward, up to Indy.

Indy grinned ferociously. "Hi. I hate a bully."

The guard also smiled. He'd witnessed such bravado many times; he knew it was futile.

The door opened. In walked the young Maharajah. Behind him came the boy Nainsukh, who'd recently shared Indiana's cell. The child looked different now, Indy noticed, becalmed as a ship on a windless sea. In his hands he carried a human skull.

Mola Ram turned to the Maharajah Zalim Singh. "Your Highness will witness the thief's conversion."

The Maharajah stood before Indiana with a look of concern. "You will not suffer," he reassured the thief. "I recently became of age and tasted the blood of Kali."

Indiana was not reassured. He saw Mola Ram take the skull from Nainsukh. It was a laughing skull, still covered with frayed skin, its nose half-rotted away, eyes nearly gutted, leathery tongue flapping out askew. Mola Ram brought the skull over to Indy.

The huge guard grabbed Indy's face, forced his head back against the slope of Death's breast, and forced his mouth open.

Before Indiana knew what was happening, or had a chance to react, the High Priest was tipping the gruesome skull forward, pouring blood from its mouth, cascading down the sluice of its tongue . . . into Indy's mouth.

Shorty screamed from across the room. "Don't drink, Indy! Spit it out!" He cried with all his spirit to Huan-t'ien, Supreme Lord of the Dark Heaven, who lived in the northern sky, to drive the evil winds from this room; he cried to The Shadow, who knew what lurked in hearts like these; he cried for immediate deliverance; and he just cried.

Indy was disoriented for a moment. He'd been expecting torture, or magic spells, but not drinking. He gagged on the foul liquid before he spat it out all over Mola Ram.

The High Priest backed off in anger. Warm blood dripped down his face, over his mouth. He licked his lips. He spoke to the Maharajah in Hindi.

Zalim Singh took a small doll from his pocket. The figurine wore pants, and a tiny rough-hewn hat. Its skin was lighter than the skin of most local dolls; the features painted carefully on its face appeared decidedly Western. It looked arguably like Indiana Jones.

The Maharajah held it up to Indy's face, to show him, then wiped the doll over Indy's body, where it soaked up his sweat and dirt and fleshy oils. And then the Maharajah began to dip the doll in and out of the flames that rose from the pot of coals in the corner.

Into the fire went the doll...and into spasms of pain went Indy. His body felt aflame, as if his very brain were being consumed. He screamed, he screamed.

"Dr. Jones!" wailed Shorty. Just to watch such a horror contorted the boy's heart nearly to stopping. He let out a series of Chinese invectives, ran up, kicked the Maharajah hard. The little monarch fell, dropping the doll. Indy slumped forward.

Short Round dove for Indy's whip, but was thrown down to the floor by one of the guards. Mola Ram gave commands. The chief guard picked up Indy's whip.

Indiana was unchained momentarily, then was

turned around and rechained facing the statue, pressed to it, his cheek pushed down on its horrid, bloodsticky breast, his gaze staring directly up into its gargoyle face.

He felt a cold noise garble through his chest.

Nainsukh went to refill the skull with fresh blood. Mola Ram began to chant. Shorty picked himself up, ran at his guard, punching, but he was quickly subdued by priests, quickly strung up against the far wall, in chains.

And then the two of them were whipped. First Indy—Shorty cried to watch it. Then Shorty.

"Leave him alone, you bastards," Indiana muttered through his haze. This was the lowest. For this, he would exact a proper price.

So they left Short Round alone; went back to whipping Indy. The leather ripped through his shirt, tore open his skin. Blood was soon soaking the splayed tatters of cloth and flesh. Indy tried to keep his mind closed. He breathed harder—the candles in Death's eyes blew out. This seemed to infuriate Mola Ram even more.

"You dare not do that," the High Priest intoned. Nainsukh returned with the second skull full of blood, gave it to Mola Ram.

Indy was turned around again, once more with his back to the idol. The giant guard pried open his slack and weary mouth, and pinched shut his nose. Once again, Mola Ram poured the bloody elixir from the laughing skull into Indiana's mouth.

"The British in India will be slaughtered," said the High Priest as he poured. "Then we will overrun the Moslems and force their Allah to bow to Kali. And then the Hebrew God will fall. And finally the

Christian God will be cast down and forgotten."

He finished pouring. The guard clasped down Indy's mouth. Indy gagged, sputtered, choked, held his breath . . . and finally swallowed.

"Soon Kali Ma will rule the world," pronounced Mola Ram.

Willie stumbled through the secret tunnel entrance, back into her room. Insects covered her totally, from her flight down the caves. She knocked them off, holding her breath, doing what she had to do to save herself. And to save Indy. She'd have plenty of time later to break down—she hoped.

She managed to stagger to her feet, headed for the door, rushed out of her room. Down the corridors of the deserted palace she flew, looking for help in the lightening shadows; the dawn was not far off.

In the first open courtyard, she stopped, panting heavily. She called out. Nobody answered. Desperately, she backed down the next hallway, stifling sobs. Paintings lined the walls here; the grand portraits of the Maharajah's forebears. They seemed to be lurking, now: spying on her from another time, in this cold hour of the late night. Slowly she paraded through this sinister gauntlet. At the end, something moved in the corner of her eye. She turned . . . one of the faces! She gasped—it was a mirror.

But then the face was behind her in the mirror, moving again. She whirled once more, her hand ready to strike. It was only Chattar Lal, the Prime Minister.

"Oh, my God, you scared me!" Willie exhaled with relief. "Listen, you've got to help. We found this tunnel—" She grabbed his shoulder, for support, and to try to communicate the urgency of the situation to him.

Captain Blumburtt rounded the corner at that moment. He nodded politely to Willie, but spoke to Chattar Lal. "Jones isn't in his room." Then, to Willie, "Miss Scott, my troops are leaving at dawn, if you'd like us to escort you as far as Delhi."

Willie felt pale. "No, you can't go! Something awful's happened. They've got Short Round and I think Indy's been—"

"What?" blurted Blumburtt.

Willie nodded excitedly. "We found a tunnel that leads to a temple below the palace! Please, come with me, I'll show you!"

The two men exchanged dubious looks. Outraged, frustrated, unraveling, Willie clutched Blumburtt by the arm and began running down the hall to her room.

Chattar Lal accompanied them. "Miss Scott, you're not making any sense," he said condescendingly.

Her teeth started chattering. "Hurry. I'm afraid they'll kill them. We saw horrible things down there—a human sacrifice. They dragged in this poor man, and this other man reached into his chest and ripped out his heart." She covered her face with her hand, to make the image go away. The two men looked at each other even more skeptically.

"Who?" pursued Blumburtt with the utmost tact.

"The priest," she rasped. "They've taken Short Round, and Indy's gone—I don't know where Indy's gone. Right beneath my bedroom there's this gigantic cathedral—a temple of death. There's some kind of cult down there, with the sacred stones Indy was searching for."

Chattar Lal smiled indulgently. "I sense the fumes of opium in all this. Perhaps Miss Scott picked up the habit in Shanghai?"

She became furious. "What're you talking about? I'm not a dope fiend! I saw it! I'll show you!"

She pulled them into her suite. "There—it's still there! She pointed to the dark opening in her wall. "There: I told you!" she hissed in triumph.

Blumburtt picked up an oil lamp, held it toward the covert entryway ... when suddenly Indiana emerged, flicking a beetle from his lapel.

Indy smiled faintly. "What's this, hide and seek?"

They were all a bit startled by his unexpected presence. Willie's shock melted instantly to relief, though. She ran to Indy, put her arms around him, felt ready to collapse.

"Oh, Indy, you got away," she wept. "Tell them what happened, they won't believe me."

She trembled in his powerful arms. He walked her to the bed, sat down there with her. Physically and emotionally exhausted, she let him take over without an argument.

"It's okay," he whispered into her hair. "You're all right now."

"They think I'm insane," she sniffled. "Tell them I'm not, Indy. Please, help me."

The awful events of the night had taken their toll. Willie sobbed into Indiana's chest, quaking, desolate.

Indy laid her down on the satin covers, stroked her cheek, brushed the hair from her face. "Hey, I thought you were supposed to be a real trouper.

Willie?" He wiped the tears away.

She held his hand. "What?" she whispered. He was here now; she was safe. She could let go.

"You've got to go to sleep now."

"I want to go home," she answered, letting her eyes close. The mattress felt so soft, his voice so deep, his hand...

"I don't blame you," he soothed. "This hasn't been what you'd call a fun vacation."

She smiled despite herself, as he continued caressing her cheek. She could feel herself sliding effortlessly to sleep. It was almost...a miracle: Indy was saving her. She'd never had such a sense of total well-being, unencumbered tranquility. It was as if she were floating placidly down, on the sound of his voice: like a child, lost in an enchantment. She felt wrapped in the safety of his nearness. She felt blissful. Serene.

Entranced.

Indiana stood. He joined Blumburtt and Chattar Lal in the hallway outside Willie's room. The Prime Minister led the way to the verandah.

First light was breaking over the mountain peaks. Orange rays highlighted the lowlying clouds; the air was crisp, expectant. In the valley below, they could see the cavalry troops readying their horses and trucks.

Indy breathed deeply the rare spirit of dawn. "I've spent my life crawling around in caves and tunnels." He shook his head, remonstrating himself. "I shouldn't have let somebody like Willie go in there with me."

Blumburtt nodded, as if he'd suspected this all along. "Miss Scott panicked?"

Indy shrugged. "When she saw the insects, she passed out cold. I carried her back to her room. She was sound asleep when I reentered the tunnel to look around some more."

"And as she slept," suggested Chattar Lal, "she undoubtedly had nightmares."

Indy looked at the Prime Minister and nodded, speaking with complete understanding in his voice. "Nightmares, yes."

"The poor child," commiserated Lal.

Indy went on nodding. "Then she must have jumped awake, not realized she was dreaming, and run out of her room. And you found her."

Blumburtt squinted at the sun rising gently over his little corner of the British Empire. "Did you discover anything in that tunnel, Dr. Jones?"

Indiana stared into the same sun, but it rose over a different quadrant of the universe for him now. "Nothing," he replied. "Just a dead end. That tunnel's been deserted for years."

From far below them a sergeant-major shouted up that the troops were ready for departure. Blumburtt waved acknowledgement.

"Well, Mr. Prime Minister," the Captain assured, "my report will duly note that we found nothing unusual here in Pankot."

Chattar Lal bowed with respect for the Crown's wise decision. "I'm sure that will please the Maharajah, Captain."

Blumburtt turned one last time to Indy. "As I said before, Dr. Jones, we'd be happy to escort you to Delhi."

Indiana smiled serenely. "Thanks, but I don't think Willie is ready to travel yet."

* * *

Dust swirled in the valley as the British army moved out, across the lowest pass. Foot soldiers, horse cavalry, supply trucks. Captain Blumburtt headed the ranks, seated in an open car. Bringing up the rear was a troop of Highland Pipers beating out a stately tattoo on the pipes and drums.

In a short time they were winding slowly down the other side of the mountain, leaving Pankot Palace to its own.

Willie half woke to the dirgelike whine of the fading bagpipes. She wasn't certain if she was dreaming or not; it was such a muted, eerie sound.

Through the mosquito netting that hung all around the bed, she saw the door to her room open. It was still dim, with the curtain drawn, but she could make out Indiana's form softly approach. She smiled. He'd come for her at last.

She shifted her position slightly as he sat down on the edge of the mattress. He remained that way, his back to her, shoulders slumped. Poor man; he must be exhausted.

She stared through the gauzy netting at the back of his head, his tousled hair. "Indy? Did you talk to them?"

"Yes," he said.

"So now they believe me," she filled in the blank.

"Yes, they believe you," he echoed.

His voice registered in a strange monotone. *He must be more ragged out than I thought*, she thought. *My turn to be gentle with him.* "Then they'll send the soldiers down into the temple," she said aloud.

He didn't say anything. She hoped he hadn't just fallen asleep right there where he was sitting; though if he had, she'd understand. She'd just pull him right down where he belonged. "I was scared to death last night," she admitted, "when I thought they were going to kill you."

"No, they won't kill me."

She laid her hand on his back. It felt moist, through his shirt, through the netting. She smiled, lovingly reproachful. "You know, you've been nothing but trouble since I hooked up with you. But I have to admit, I'd miss you if I lost you."

Slowly, Indiana started to turn. "You won't lose me, Willie."

She pulled her hand back; her fingers were viscid with blood.

His face came around until it was staring straight at her. The netting hung between them, a diaphanous veil, but even so, she could see the change in his eyes.

His eyes, normally so deep, so clear, flecked with coppery gold, crystal-pure—his eyes had undergone some indescribable transformation. Something about them was opaque now. Tarnished. It made her cold. Viscerally ill. She shuddered.

She had lost him.

Morning services began in the temple of death. A sea of lurid faces swayed to the droning of the winds in the subterranean cathedral. The sacrificial chant grew slowly, organically, feeding on its own rumble and wail.

Among the worshippers the young Maharajah sat on a low, raised platform at the edge of the crevasse, staring across the fuming chasm toward the altar of Kali Ma.

"Jai ma Kali, jai ma Kali..."

Once again, the three Sankara Stones glowed magically at the feet of the demon goddess. Mola

Ram materialized out of the swirling smokes that shrouded the altar; he, too, was chanting.

"Jai ma Kali, jai ma Kali..."

Female acolytes appeared from side chambers, swathed in red tunics. They passed along the row of somber priests, and painted lines on their foreheads, as Mola Ram began addressing the audience in Sanskirt.

Chattar Lal, dressed in robes, stood beside Indiana, to the left of the altar. An acolyte drew the devotional markings on Lal's forehead. Indiana stared vacantly into the liquid flames at the bottom of the pit. He was living the Nightmare now.

Liquid flames at the bottom of the pit scudded across the surface, leapt up twisting, turned into dark birds that fluttered insanely, looking for somewhere to roost. Higher, they flew, flapping against each other and the stone walls, screeching out of the pit... and into his head.

No brainstuff in there now, only a vast, umbrageous cavern: murky, with these large birds flapping. They didn't seem to be able to land, they just kept beating their wings against the inside of his skull.

Shadows whispered in this lingering midnight.

Somewhere, a nocturne dawdled over the lower registers, nearly off-key.

Somewhere, a candle guttered.

He moved, without moving: back, in time, in space, an hour, a dungeon, a bloodthirst, a black-song, turning through pitchy tunnels brilliant with death, painlit and tomb-ridden, emerging into Willie's chamber, spilling from the stony wound. What's this, hide and seek?

Willie was there, the sorceress, entwining her ten-

drils around his back; her fingers were flaming talons gouging his flesh. Oh Indy you got away, she said, tell that what happened they won't believe me. Her hair was afire, her mouth a treacherous cavity without bottom, her tongue a salamander, her eyes icy mirrors reflecting the face of his own dusky soul.

He walked her to the bed, her flaming hair spattered his cheek. The birds in his head fluttered wildly, scraping the inner table of skull with their craggy beaks.

It's okay you're all right now.

They think I'm insane tell them I'm not Indy please help me.

Her salamander tongue lashed out as she leaned her head down against his body. Her sobs covered the sound of its gnawing: the lizard was taking great bites from his flesh, chewing open his chest.

He laid her down on the covers, hey I thought you were supposed to be a real trouper Willie, tears streamed down her cheeks, tears of blood, he touched them and they turned to lava, burning through his fingers to the bone, white bone gaping in the somber wind.

What? she whispered.

You've got to go to sleep now.

The serpent in her mouth had chewed down to his ribs now, crunching on his breastbone. I want to go home, the serpent was saying.

Its home was in his chest.

I don't blame you this hasn't been what you'd call a fun vacation. The snake slithered into his chest, curled up, slept there.

The sorceress slept.

The birds fluttered.

He joined Blumburtt and Chattar Lal on the ve-

*randah. Blumburtt had no face. The sun broke over
the peaks in a bloody mist. Lal spoke, but the words
came out of Indy's mouth, like a gaseous exhala-
tion.*

*I've spent my life crawling around in caves and
tunnels I shouldn't have let somebody like Willie go
in there with me.*

The faceless captain nodded.

*When she saw the insects she passed out cold I
carried her back to her room she was sound asleep
when I re-entered the tunnel to look around some
more.*

*The serpent shifted positions in his chest, re-
curled, settled back into uneasy slumber.*

*And as she slept she undoubtedly had night-
mares.*

Nightmares. Yes.

The poor child.

*Two of the lightless birds tangled, brawled, tum-
bled to the base of his skull, lay there flapping on
their backs, wounded, terrified.*

*Did you discover anything in that tunnel Dr.
Jones?*

Nothing.

Just a dead end.

Deserted.

*The deserted hollows in his skull echoed; the
echoes of broken feathers, scratching the stone.
Empty, obscure. The birds had left.*

But I don't think Willie is ready to travel yet.

*He returned to her room. She still slept there,
the sorceress, curled in her bed.*

In his chest, the serpent stirred.

*The sorceress awoke. He sat beside her. He faced
away, that she could not see the shredded tissue of*

*his breast, the ragged hole through which the reptile
had crawled to nestle by his heart.*

Indy?

Yes.

So now they believe me.

*Yes they believe you. You leave us no doubt.
Sorceress with flaming hair you will die before I let
you rouse the beast within my chest.*

I thought they were going to kill you.

No they won't kill me.

*She drew her talons down his back, tearing skin,
calling forth blood.*

You won't lose me.

*He turned, stared into her mirror eyes, saw him-
self: man of smoke, laced with horror, oozing blood,
trying to still the serpent, listening for echoes in the
dusk, waiting for the shattering scream.*

The serpent twisted.

From the distance came a flapping.

Indiana continued to stare into the liquid flames
at the bottom of the pit as Mola Ram spoke. Chattar
Lal translated the High Priest's speech to Indiana.
"Mola Ram is telling the faithful of our victory. He
says the British have left the palace, which proves
Kali Ma's new power."

Indy nodded hypnotically. "Yes, I understand."
He understood well.

Mola Ram finished orating. The intonations resumed. The wind howled, the sulfuric fumes billowed and thinned.

Indiana rocked on his heels, staring up at the
divinely inspired idol beside him.

Beneath the temple, in the dark of the mine, children dug at the earth with bleeding fingers. Fat guards

flogged malingerers, or those too sickly to go on, with leather straps. The earth crumbled sometimes; children were buried alive or crushed in the rubble or maimed or suffocated.

Short Round worked here now. He sweated next to the others, the lost children, clawing at the rocks, seeking the last two Sankara Stones. Chained at the ankles, they toiled, praying to die; doomed.

Short Round and five others were starting a new tunnel when the finality of the situation began to sink in. The weight of this knowledge—the agony of the remainder of the short life of Short Round— hit him squarely, sat him down in the dirt. What could it all mean? Had he offended some god or ancestor? What would Indy do now? But he couldn't count on Indy anymore. Indy had drunk the evil potion that had turned him from Dr. Jones to Mr. Hyde. Indy was lost.

Shorty appealed to the Celestial Ministry of Time, to contract the length of his stay here. He sat on the ground, near tears; picked up a handful of dirt, let it sift through his fingers. "Grounded out," he whispered.

He didn't sit for long. A leather thong flayed his back; only the hot shock of it prevented him from screaming in pain. The guard moved on; Shorty got back to work.

He and two others strained at a large rock wedged in the wall, blocking the way the tunnel was to go. They pulled, they levered it; finally it gave. It came loose, rolled down a short incline—and Short Round gave an involuntary shout.

They'd exposed a vein of molten lava. Thick with itself, barely moving, it hissed like a wary cobra.

The children shouted, pointing until the guard

came; then he whipped them brutally for being so stupid and noisy. His eyes reflected the glowing venom of the nearby vein.

Suddenly the small fissure spurted out a tiny bubble of steam, spewing a fine spray of lava over the guard's legs.

He shrieked, fell to the ground, tried to rub the melting ore off his skin. The odor of burning flesh filled the tunnel.

As the children watched him, a strange thing happened. His face actually relaxed, shed its hardened edges. His eyes, which had so easily reflected the blood-tones in the lava just a moment before, now dimmed with human frailty, and seemed to come alive. To remember.

He stopped moaning; his eyes came to focus on Short Round. The man looked almost thankful; he seemed on the verge of tears, as if realizing he'd only been having a nightmare and now he was awake.

He pleaded forgiveness to Short Round—in Hindi, then in English.

Other guards appeared suddenly. They grabbed this fallen comrade, dragged him out of the tunnel. He struggled against them, though, trying to break away. Trying to stay awake.

He didn't want to return to the nightmare of Kali.

Short Round watched with dawning comprehension as the wretched guard was pulled out of sight by his brethren mindslaves. "The fire," Short Round whispered to himself. "The fire makes him wake up! I can make Dr. Jones—"

Before he finished articulating his discovery, he lifted a heavy rock. The other children observed him fearfully as he hefted it with defiance, afraid he was going to lob it at the last retreating guard, thereby earning them all more lashes. He didn't heave it at the guard, though; rather, he smashed the rock down on the leg-chains that bound him to the other kids.

The ankle-iron was rusty, he figured; it couldn't withstand all that much battering. None of the guards really expected any of the children to actually *try* to escape—after all, where could they go? Short Round smiled grimly with his newfound knowledge. Knowledge was power, Dr. Jones had always told him.

With this power, he would free Dr. Jones.

Repeatedly he brought the rock down on his rusting shackles as the other children stared nervously.

Short Round was determined to escape. And unbeknownst to the guards, he had somewhere to go.

The wind thrummed over the cavernous ceiling, joining the atonal incantations of the multitude gathered in the temple. Mola Ram warbled in counterpoint to the tumultuous chanting. The Maharajah sat upon his dais, weaving, transfixed in the smoke and fervor.

Chattar Lal still stood beside Indiana. "Do you understand what he tells us?" he prodded the neophyte.

Indiana nodded dully. "Kali Ma protects us. We are her children. We pledge devotion by worshipping her with offerings of flesh and blood."

Chattar Lal seemed pleased. His student was coming along so quickly.

A scream prevented his response though—heartrending, terrified, rising out of the fume-clogged shadows.

Indiana watched emotionlessly as Willie was brought out. She was dressed now in the skirt and halter top of a Rajput maiden, draped with jewels and flowers; held fast by two priests, she wailed, struggling to break free, sweating, crying, swearing, spitting: she knew the fate that awaited.

Chattar Lal motioned toward her to Indy. "Your friend has *seen*, and she had *heard*. Now she will not *talk*."

As she was dragged before the statue of Kali, she saw Indiana. "Indy! Help me! For God's sake what's the matter with you!"

Indy stared at her impassively while her wrists were manacled to the square iron frame that hung from the tireless arms of the fearsome stone goddess.

The sorceress hissed at him Indy help me for god's sake what's the matter with you, but he could only smile at her treachery. Everything was red now, but in negative, so what was dark was light and what was light was dark; but all red. Except the sorceress: she was black.

Black and buzzing, as if ten thousand hornets comprised her substance. Zzzzzzzzhhhh, she screamed at him.

Ssshhh, he thought, you'll wake the serpent. But Kali was here, now. Kali's inspiration alone would quiet the buzzing, still the serpent in his chest. Only through pain and torture and sacrifice to Kali Ma would the buzzing cease, would the serpent sleep.

Indy looked down at his feet. A live boa constrictor slithered over the stone floor, heading for someplace dark. Indy stooped, picked it up, caressed its head: they were spiritbrothers, now. He held the snake to his chest, near its cousin who slept there—held it so Willie could see him with his new family.

She couldn't believe what was happening. "Indy," she begged. "Don't let them do this to me. Don't do this." But he didn't move a muscle to help her. He just kept petting the damn snake.

She was going to die.

She was going to die horribly. Painfully. Alone.

They had taken hold of him somehow; she could see that clearly enough. But how? He'd always been too arrogant for his own good, but she'd actually found that kind of cute—sometimes, at least. Could arrogance account for this...possession? Possessed, that's how he looked.

Or maybe this was just the final stage of a powerful seduction, seduced by the fortune and glory he was always after. She could understand seduction—those diamonds were certainly alluring—but this seemed a little over the edge.

Magic?

She didn't know, or care. She only knew she was about to die, and she didn't know why and didn't want to, and hated him for it, and was afraid.

The priests shackled her ankles to the basket.

"Stop it, you're hurting me!" she screamed. "You big lousy dirty ape." Rage foamed at her lips, then dissolved again into supplication. "Be nice, fellas. Come on." And when this had no effect, the distress call again: "Indy!"

Mola Ram circled her as the front of the frame was closed, wedging her, spread-eagled, in the wafer-thin cage. Indiana looked away from her, to gaze adoringly at the face of the monstrous goddess above them. He dropped his snake to the floor; it crawled into a corner.

The priests tore off Willie's necklaces.

"You got some kind of nerve!" she roared. "I

knew you thugs were just a bunch of cheapskates! You're saving these trinkets for someone—well, she'll never look as good as me!" She was defiant now, contemptuous.

Mola Ram came before her. He seemed pleased with her insolence. He bowed slightly, then raised his hand, tauntingly, toward her heart.

Icy chills coursed through her, to watch the High Priest's fingers approach her chest. She'd seen this part before; it terrorized her to envision it now. Her knees turned to water. If she hadn't been held up by shackles and meshing she'd have crumpled to the ground. All her fine brazen boldness shriveled in the face of this wizard's advancing hand. She fell to bargaining. "Wait. Not yet. Please. I'll do anything. I know a lot of politicians and important industrialists. I was a personal dinner guest of Chiang Kai Shek. I know people who work for Al Capone." A surrealistic thought struck her, and she laughed absurdly. "In fact, do you have a cousin named Frank Nitti, he lives in Chicago, you know you could be his brother."

Mola Ram sneered at her rantings. Heinously, he brought his hand closer. She felt his icicle fingers touch the cloth over her breast. There was a sickening pressure, like a finger pushing into a throat, or a thumb over an eye: nauseating pressure, intrusive, unexpected, violating.

She swooned.

In the half-lit tunnel, Short Round set a measured beat, stone against iron, trying to crack his bonds. He'd seen it done just this way in *I Am a Fugitive from a Chain Gang*, except it was harder to do than to watch. His arm was growing tired, his despair strong. What would Indy and Willie do without him? What if the Wheel of Transmigration separated them in the next life? It well might; there was no predicting the roll of the Wheel.

The other children continued to watch him. He wouldn't have minded some help, but they looked so weird standing there—like ghosts, or worse—that he decided concentrating on his task was the best bet. He thrust his fatigued arm down one more time, knocking stone against iron. And the clasp broke. Just like that: he was free.

The other children stared darkly at him, in wonder, in disbelief, in unanticipated *new* belief. This was freedom, here, in their midst.

Furtively, Short Round peered about. He was out of bondage none too soon, it seemed. At the tunnel mouth, a guard was approaching. In the torch-lit shadows, Short Round took a chance. He dove, rolled across the tunnel to a mine car full of rocks being pushed along the rails by two chained slaves.

The guard lumbered past, unsuspecting. Using the mine car as cover, Short Round crouched, walking along with it, up and out of the pit.

The other children from his chain gang watched him escape, but said nothing.

Up in the temple, Willie came out of her swoon to see Mola Ram walking away. He hadn't plucked out her heart; he'd just been toying with her! Tears of hope sprang to her eyes. Maybe all wasn't lost yet.

She struggled fiercely to break her bonds, pulled and tugged at her wrists—and good God, it happened: with all the lubricating sweat, she managed to extricate one slender wrist from the manacle that strapped her to the sacrificial frame.

She reached out her free left arm imploringly to Indiana. "Indy, help us! Snap out of it. You're not one of them. Please. Please come back to me. Please, come back to me."

Indy walked over to her cage, reached out slowly, took her hand in his. She grasped his fingers tightly. He brought her hand up to his lips, kissed it. They stared deeply into each other's eyes. *Yes, yes,* Willie thought, *he's come for me.*

Resolutely he lifted her hand back to the iron frame, wrapped the shackle around her wrist, snapped it shut, locked the cage door in place. Then he bestowed a knowing look upon Mola Ram, who smiled, nodded, began chanting again.

Willie was aghast. "No. What're you doing? Are you mad?"

He just stared at her, as if from a long way away.

She spat at him. She had never hated anyone so much. She would not beg again. She hoped he burned in hell.

The sorceress-demon spat: from her black mouth, it sparked and flared. The buzzing was intensely loud now. It almost drowned out the fluttering, which had returned. The spit seared like fire, hissing in the flesh of his face, hissing with the serpent in his chest, the serpent awake now, uncoiling...

But Kali would put it to rest. If he only gave himself to Kali, lost himself in Kali, quelled the buzzing fluttering hissing with the soporific drone of the name of Kali Ma.

Calmly, hollowly, he wiped her spittle from his face; walked away from her, joined the congregation in its febrile chanting: "Mola Ram, Sunda Ram, jai ma Kali, jai ma Kali..."

Chattar Lal and Mola Ram exchanged a satisfied glance, gladdened at the sight of the cold-hearted betrayal.

The chanting grew louder.

The wind blasted on, its abominable yowl.

Short Round raced up the next tunnel, then flattened himself against a wall, panting. He peeked around the corner. Just as he'd remembered: this was one of the holding caves. There on the floor in one corner were Indy's whip, hat, and bag. He ran in, picked the things up; put the hat on his head, the bullwhip on his belt, the bag over his shoulder... and felt, for all the world, like a miniature Indiana Jones. He pulled himself erect and marched upright into the adjacent tunnel. There, two guards saw him. They immediately gave chase.

Now he *really* felt like Indiana Jones. He tore out into this level of the excavation, running full throttle, dodging guards, outdistancing his lumbering pursuers, weaving among the scores of slave-children who watched this elusive boy in amazement.

He darted in a narrow side tunnel, losing the guards on his tail. Up a twisting shaft, Short Round climbed, coming out on another level. Stealthily he crawled through an access tunnel; warily he peered back into the main pit.

Twenty yards away, he saw a tall, wooden ladder leaning against the wall, its top perched against a ledge that fronted a warren of burrows. Other tunnels pierced the rockface up and down the length of the ladder. From the lowest of these, a child emerged, carrying a sack of rocks. He stepped out onto the ladder, climbed down carrying his load.

When the boy reached the bottom, he nearly collapsed from exhaustion—then jumped in shock to see Short Round running toward him at top speed. Shorty motioned him to keep quiet. Incredulous, the boy simply gaped at Short Round as the furtive escapee leapt to the ladder and began to scramble up. Just like James Cagney in the last scene of *Public Enemy*. Short Round hoped it wasn't going to be his own last scene, as well.

He was already fairly high when the guard spotted him. The guard chased him up the ladder. Children in nearby alcoves stopped working to watch as Short Round ascended higher and higher, the angry guard closing the distance between them.

Twenty feet above the top of the ladder, a wide overhang of rock jutted out far into the center of the great pit. Twenty feet out from the wall against which the ladder teetered, a rope hung in space, straight down from the overlying shelf, dangling from a small hole in that partial ceiling.

Dirty faces stared up at Short Round from every nook and burrow as he reached the top of the ladder. The guard was barely ten feet behind him. Shorty climbed off the ladder into the tunnel at the top...then a moment later, with a running jump, leapt back onto it, kicking it away from the wall.

He held on tightly—so did the guard, several rungs lower—as the ladder tipped in a gentle arc, away from the wall, out into the open pit. Certain suicide. At least that was the thought of the mesmerized children who watched the scene being played out. They wished him well in his final escape from this place.

But as the top of the ladder passed the bottom of the hanging rope, Short Round grabbed onto it. The ladder, with the guard, continued on over, crashing thunderously to the earth far below—while Short Round dangled precariously in space for a moment, then steadily pulled himself up the rope, through the roof hole, into the overhead chamber.

He rolled a few feet across the floor; he lay still. It was empty in here, and quiet, though in the next room he could hear the muffled droning of a thousand narcotized voices. It was a disturbing sound.

He got up, went to the far door, pushed it open a crack.

Red light flared around the black statue of Kali, into the small room behind the altar of the temple of death.

In the temple, chains clanked, gears ground, as the sacrificial frame was raised, then supinated, then up-ended, and flipped over, until Willie, stretched out on the iron bracing, found herself staring face-down into the bubbling lava pit.

Staring at her own death. How excruciating it would be; how meaningless. How alone: that was the worst. Periodically she caught an image of herself in the glistening curvatures of the red bubbles far below, forming, breaking, distorting her reflection until it burst. Reflections of her life: contorted, overheated, now about to explode, like a droplet of water in a vat of acid. She wished she could do it over; she'd do it differently next time.

But there wouldn't be a next time. She didn't believe in karma, or reincarnation, or heaven, or miracles. It would take a miracle now to save her.

She held her breath. She hoped she passed out before it got too painful.

Mola Ram gave orders to the executioner, who slowly turned the giant wooden wheel that lowered the basket. The crowd chanted. Willie screamed. Indy turned to watch.

The sorceress hung above the pit in her true form, that of giant raven, suspended floating on the hot-air currents above the hole of fire. She was not flapping or fluttering now, as she had against the inside of his skull. She only floated, now: smiling, buzzing softly, knowing. Knowing the horror. The emptiness of his skull. The poison in his chest. She knew. She knew it all.

She had to die.

Mola Ram joined in the chanting now; the chanting got wilder. Indiana lent his voice to the masses.

Willie hung, suspended on the iron frame, watching the boiling magma draw nearer to her body, as it was lowered, inch by inch, into the sacrificial pit. Into the fire.

8

Break for Freedom

Short Round peered from behind the altar, into the cavernous temple, just in time to see Willie being dipped. And there, at the crater's edge, stood Indiana, impassively watching her disappear.

Shorty whispered to himself. "Indy, no."

The chanting was so loud it almost drowned out his thought. But he knew what he had to do. He had to be Indy's pinchhitter. He had to wake Indy up. He had to pull Willie out. He had to get to America, and that was no big joke.

But first things first. He promised the Three Star-Gods a shrine in his heart forever, in return for success on this mission. He promised Lou Gehrig never to doubt the great slugger's batting average again, even if his brother Chu came back as a whole herd of baby elephants.

He laid Indy's accessories down on the shadow

of an archway; he turned his baseball cap brim-backwards for action; and he jumped out onto the altar.

He waved at Indy. Chattar Lal saw him first, though. The Prime Minister shouted at two guards to grab the kid, but the kid was too fast. As the guards tried to apprehend him, he scooted off the altar toward Indiana.

One of the priests intervened, grabbing Short Round by the arm. Shorty bit the man's hand; the priest let go. Another priest got in the way. Short Round kicked him hard, then skirted his crippled lunge.

In another second, he made it to Indy. He smiled up hopefully: maybe the good doctor was already awake, was just putting on a good act as part of a clever con game, to fool these fools into something foolhardy.

Indy brutally backhanded Short Round across the face. He fell to the ground, his hat knocked off.

Tears coated his eyes. "Wake *up*, Dr. Jones."

Blood trickled from the corner of Short Round's mouth as he stared at his hero in wounded disbelief. The moment didn't last long, however; it only forged, for Shorty, the notion of what he had to do. It would be hard for him, but what, in this life, was not hard?

He sprang up, ran toward the wall. Another guard was quickly on his heels.

Chattar Lal had observed this entire transaction with distinct approval: the great Indiana Jones was now an obvious convert and devout believer. Satisfaction filled the Prime Minister's eyes as he watched the guard chase down the annoying child, and as he watched Willie creak down to her final consumption.

Willie continued to try holding her breath on the descending frame, but it was no use. It was impossibly hot, immeasurably bright. Waves of heat rose to scald her face; the acid fumes burned her eyes, her lungs, her skin. She was going to die.

It was lonely. And scary. She tried to think of a prayer, but couldn't think. She tried to twist away from the searing pain, but couldn't move. Except she kept moving closer.

Short Round, meanwhile, reached the wall, where he yanked a flaming torch out of its bracket, and swiveled on his attacker. The firebrand whisked past the guard's face, backing him off. Shorty ran up to the executioner, swinging the torch fiercely. The executioner retreated from his wheel; Willie hung, suspended where she was, temporarily unmoving.

Mola Ram was not as sanguine about these events as Chattar Lal seemed to be. This little monster was defiling the rites of Kali: he had to be punished. "Catch him! Kill him!" the High Priest shouted in Hindi, enraged.

Two more guards went after Short Round, who was once more running straight at Indy.

"Indy, wake up!" he yelled again. No response. At the last second he turned on the two guards about to catch him, forcing them back with his torch. In that second, Indy grabbed him from behind and began to strangle him.

Indy held Shorty by the neck, lifting and turning the boy in the air until they were facing each other, at Indy's arm's length. Short Round gasped for breath, turning blue, as Indiana choked the life out of him.

The serpent hissed and rattled in his chest, angered at the rude awakening. It had sensed the de-

mon-child's attack before Indy had actually seen him. By the time the demon approached with the torch, Indy was ready, the serpent was ready. Ready to strike.

Indy wake up! the demon-child screamed, the words etched in the torchlight he cradled. The serpent recoiled. The demon was protean: he transformed into a ruby clot of blood, thick with purpose, gelid and steaming in the cold cave air, smelling juicy with death.

Spinning, sputtering ... Indy grabbed it, this clot-thing demon-child. Grabbed it and squeezed, tried to squeeze the dark squirting gob into something of a more pleasing shape, something the shape of Kali, something the size of his fist. Twisting, molding, forming, he turned the thing in his hands, turned it around and around until it faced him, its ghastly eyes bulging out of the gelatinous mass, waving its fire, facing his screaming, calling to the serpent.

With his last breath the boy croaked, "Indy, I love you," uttered the name of the Caretaker of the Celestial Ministry of Exorcism, and thrust the flaming torch into Indy's side.

Indiana went down, the fire roasting his flesh. He wailed in pain, letting go of Short Round.

Fire filled his head, raging out of control in the empty caverns. The serpent shrieked, uncoiling, writhing. The demon-child called to it: it called back, angry with new memory.

Short Round held the torch fast against Indiana's flank, until a guard finally grabbed him, knocking the torch away.

Indiana writhed in pain on the ground. *The light was blinding.* The chanting started to crescendo. The executioner returned to his wheel, began lowering Willie once more. Chattar Lal smiled. Mola Ram praised Kali. The guard drew a knife, brought it up to Short Round's throat. "Hold it," said Indiana, rising. "He's mine." Indy took Shorty from the assassin, carried him a few steps away, lifted him into the air, held him high over the pit. Short Round looked down into the boiling furnace in terror; then into Indy's eyes, for the last time.

Indy winked.

"I'm all right," he whispered. "You ready?"

Shorty winked back.

He threw Short Round to a clear area, turned, and punched the nearest priest in the face; then punched another in the belly. Short Round gave one nearby guard a whirling karate kick to the side. At the same moment, a priest attacked. Shorty grabbed the cleric's belt, rolled onto his own back, and flipped the man onto his head. The crowd beyond the crevasse was all wrapped up in the ecstasy of the ritual; they had no idea what was going on around the stone goddess. Chattar Lal knew well; he quickly exited behind the altar as the fighting increased.

Two priests converged on Indy, but Short Round threw himself in front of one, who consequently flipped into the other. Indy threw another priest into the executioner. Both went flying down off the platform. Unfortunately, the executioner disengaged the handbrake. The iron cage containing Willie started plummeting down the pit.

Indy jumped on the platform, clamping the brake on the spinning wheel. Again Willie stopped in her deathly plunge.

Mola Ram was growing more disturbed. He moved carefully through the disorder, toward the Sankara Stones on the altar.

Another priest attacked Indy, swinging his incense burner. Indy doubled over, then stood up under the priest, letting the man's own momentum carry him over, and into the crevasse. There was a hissing flash; the priest was no more.

Short Round stood with his back to a wall, holding several guards at bay with a torch in one hand, a knife in the other.

The executioner crawled to his wheel, went back to lowering Willie. She was only yards away from the spumes of fulminating lava now. The heat was so intense, her clothes began to smoke; her eyelashes began to singe. Her consciousness reached the limits of its strength; her life began to shimmer. Random images flitted through her cooking brain; ancient memories, silvered feelings. The last thought that trickled by before she blacked out entirely was, *In olden days a glimpse...*

Indy knocked the executioner off the platform once more. As he was beginning to crank the cage up out of the brew, a priest attacked him with a pole. He grabbed the pole, threw the priest off its other end, into the pit.

He fenced a guard with the pole, finally bashing him unconscious. This brought him near the altar, where he noticed Mola Ram bending over the stones. Indy broke the stick over Ram's back.

Mola Ram fell forward. Indy raised his half-stick to finish the job on Ram, when the High Priest looked up, smiled... and disappeared through a secret trapdoor at the base of the altar.

Indy swore, threw the stick away, raced back to the wheel, and began to crank it, once more slowly raising the cage in which Willie's unconscious body was still trapped, still smoking.

Chattar Lal appeared behind him, dagger upraised.

"Indy, look out!" shouted Short Round, still swinging his torch.

Indy turned in time to dodge Lal's dagger thrust; the two men struggled beside the wheel. Below, the iron frame creaked lower; the brake was on, but worn thin.

By now the congregation across the crevasse could see something was awry. They stopped chanting, began dispersing in increasing panic. The little Maharajah was one of the first to leave, surrounded by a cadre of his bodyguards.

Indy, breaking free from Chattar Lal, managed to hold the wheel steady. Lal attacked him again. Indy blocked the knife, stunning Lal, knocking him against the wheel.

The wheel turned; Chattar Lal was caught in its spokes. His leg was partially crushed in the gears; but he managed to free himself, and crawled away.

Shorty jumped up on the platform, holding the last guard back with his torch as Indy once more put the brake on—though it didn't feel like it would hold for long. Then Indy stood up, but the guard ran away. Indy and Shorty frantically began turning the wheel, raising the cage.

When the iron frame was out of the pit, suspended at floor level, Short Round stayed at the wheel, holding it with all his strength, while Indy ran to the edge of the pit and pulled the basket over solid ground.

"Give me some slack," he called to Shorty. Short Round turned the wheel a bit; Indy lowered the cage to the earth.

He released Willie's bindings, stared anxiously at her unconscious form. "Willie, Willie. Wake up,

Willie." He could hardly remember the specifics of the Nightmare anymore, only the feeling of sickening terror, and a few flitting images: huge scavenger birds, hungry snakes (ugh! snakes!), a demonchild who was Shorty but wasn't, and Willie as a malignant sorceress bent on eating his soul. And he'd tried to kill her, he remembered, had laughed to see her lowered into the pit for Kali's pleasure. Thank God it was over; over, awake, back among the living.

Willie moaned, moved her head, fluttered her eyes.

"Willie!" he said happily.

She opened her eyes, saw him over her...and slapped him. Tried to, anyway; her hand was so weak, it barely grazed his cheek.

Shorty flinched all the same.

Indy just grinned. "Willie, it's me. I'm back, I'm back, Willie." And then he sang: "'Home, home on the range, where the deer and the antelope play.'"

Willie had never been so glad to hear such bad singing in her life. As the fresh air and foul voice revived her, she was crying, coughing, laughing, all at once. She didn't see Chattar Lal with the knife until it was almost too late.

"Look out," she choked.

Indy whirled. Falling backwards, he kicked the dagger from Lal's hand. Lal was on him in an instant.

They rolled around the floor. Willie was too weak to move; Shorty stayed by his post at the wheel.

The antagonists scuttled near the edge, then away. They pushed apart; both men stood, Indy between Lal and the pit. Willie inched away from them, toward the wheel.

Lal began wailing in Hindi: "Betray, betray, you betray Kali Ma. Kali Ma shall destroy you."

Then he lunged.

With the strength of madness, he flew into Indiana, attempting to take Indy with him in a glorious suicidal plunge.

He knocked both of them back onto the sacrificial frame. Their combined momentum scraped it along the floor, swung it out over the pit, where it dangled precariously.

Indy broke from Lal's grip, leaping away, slamming against the inner upper lip of the shaft, hanging on to the precipice . . . as Willie threw off the brake with all her returning strength. The crankwheel whined, and the frame sank like pig iron.

Fell and tumbled, with Chattar Lal riding it all the way.

The splash of molten lava. To Willie, it sounded like sweet revenge.

Indy looked down. Chattar Lal's body briefly exploded into flame. The flesh was gone in an instant; there was a momentary glimpse of skeleton; and then all was consumed and obliterated by the broil.

Indiana pulled himself back to safety. Willie sat up; Shorty ran over. They huddled there a moment, quiet, in each other's arms. Glad to rest, to be together, to be alive.

The temple was empty now, and silent, except for the bodies of unconscious priests and the hissing of the liquid fires.

Indy walked over to the three Sankara Stones at the base of the altar. They weren't glowing anymore. Shorty brought his bundle over to him: hat, whip, bag, shirt. Indy put the stones in his bag, the bag over his shoulder; the whip on his belt; the shirt on his wounded back.

Then he walked over to where Short Round's cap still lay on the floor. He picked it up, dusted it off, set it ceremoniously on Short Round's head.

Then he put on his own hat.

And all was right with the world.

Shorty smiled loudly at his old pal. "Indy, my friend." No matter what else happened now, that existed still, and would forever exist, like the stars.

Willie got her legs back and walked over to them. "Indy, you've got to get us out of here."

Indy looked around this place of evil, heard the distant rumblings of the mine cars full of rocks, the clandestine tortures, the whimpering of innocents. . . .

"Right. All of us," he muttered.

They moved off, toward the chamber behind the altar.

In the mines, a remarkable thing had begun to happen. The children had seen the face of freedom.

Dozens of children had actually witnessed Short Round's miraculous exploit. Then rumor of the feat had spread to scores of others:

One had escaped.

One had escaped.

One could escape.

It put an edge to their work now. They watched their guards through lowered lids, instead of lowering their heads altogether. They shuffled their feet from surliness or indecision, rather than from exhaustion. Some even counted their numbers, and the number of the guard.

When Mola Ram fled the fighting at the altar, he hurried down to the mines. He told the chief guards what was taking place. He directed some of them back up to the temple, to help with the battle; he told the rest to be on the alert for the three heathens, who might try to escape by fleeing this way, through the mines.

He told no one to be on the alert for a slave rebellion.

A chain gang of five children trudged with effort down a dark tunnel toward an empty mine car. The little girl at the end of the line fell.

The guard at the tunnel mouth saw this as an obvious case of malingering. He stormed in furiously, yanked her to her feet, raised his strap to beat her. At the top of his swing, he saw Indy rise out of a shadow. Indy crashed his fist into the guard's jaw; the guard went down and out.

Short Round took the key from the guard's belt and quickly unlocked the leg-irons on the slave-children as they stared in silent awe at these proceedings. When they were free, Indy showed them how to shackle the guard to the mine car.

That's how it began.

These five jumped another guard in another tunnel—he was so surprised he didn't even shout before he was knocked unconscious with rocks—liberating five more. And then there were ten.

It was like a chain reaction. Dozens were roaming the tunnels at will before the remaining guards even knew anything was amiss. Then it was a free-for-all.

The alarm was given. Guards tried to herd the manacled kids to a central cell. Indy stopped many, though; he'd bring one down with his whip and the free children would pelt him with stones, or he'd punch one cold and Willie or Shorty would take his keys.

Every guard that fell freed more children.

The power was infectious. Guards were on the run. Willie would crack them senseless with a spade; Shorty tripped them with chains; bands of ex-slaves pushed them from ledges or off ladders; baskets full of rocks were emptied onto the heads of fleeing guards.

Finally, the guards were just massively outnumbered by their prisoners. And, of course, outclassed.

When all were free, with the mine guards routed, the children stood in a great pack, looking around with a lot of exhilaration, and not a little surprise.

Short Round stood before them, the true inspiration for this revolt in the first place. "Come on, follow me!" he called out, leading them, cheering, toward the exit. It was a children's crusade.

Indy and Willie followed. The troop encountered an occasional guard on the way—either trying to stop them or trying to flee—but the children stormed right over them, overwhelming any opposition by sheer weight of numbers and momentum.

Up the winding path they marched, their own masters at last. Through the last tunnel, up to the top of the excavation, into the room behind the altar...

Into the temple.

Deserted now. Only the wind hummed its lonely melody; only Kali stood there to watch.

Indy, Willie, and some of the bigger children tore down a long wooden plank from the altar, one of the decorative elements flanking the giant statue, carved with myriad hideous figures of Kali and her atrocities. When it had fallen to the ground, they carried it to the edge of the natural chasm separating the altar from the rest of the temple, the last barrier to freedom.

They planted one end firmly on the edge, up-ended it—for a moment it looked as if they were erecting a flagstaff—then let it arc down across the crevasse, until its other end rested on the far precipice.

It formed a narrow plank over the churning lava.

Children kept arriving. The altar side was already filled to overflowing; kids were teetering on the brink.

Indy started them running across the plank to the other side. Below them fire bubbled, flaring with occasional outbursts of molten spray. But none of the children faltered. One by one they ran to the far side of the temple, toward the palace, toward freedom.

After a while, though, Indy noticed the plank beginning to smoke, from the constant, intense heat that rose. The children were yelping as they ran, now, the hot, dry wood scorching their bare feet. Indy sent them packing faster and faster; the wood smoldered progressively, white smoke turning black.

Finally the plank burst into flame at two points. Indy urged the last kids on, shouting them across as they leapt over the flames. The plank cracked as the last child scrambled to the other side. When Shorty stepped out onto it, it burned through completely, flaming into the pit. Indy and Willie caught him by the collar at the last moment and dragged him back from the fall.

On the other side, some children turned to wait for their deliverers.

"Go! Go!" Indy called to them.

So they went.

Out the rear exit of the temple, up a hundred twisting stairs, through a dozen secret passages, out a dozen secret entrances to the palace.

Through the palace corridors they ran, hundreds of fleeing children, wearing hundreds of unchained smiles. They crossed courtyards, crossed bridges when they came to them, crossed foyers and exterior portals and entrance ramps and gateways.

And then it was the open road, the jungle, the mountain passes.

They were free.

"Now what are we going to do?" asked Shorty as the last liberated slave-child disappeared out of the temple.

"Go the long way," Indiana suggested. As always, just making it up as he went along.

They trotted back into the room behind the altar, then on to the top of the quarry. Indy looked at one of the small, empty gondolas sitting unattended on its rails.

"Those tracks have got to lead out of the mines," he reasoned.

He moved forward, to the top of a circular path.

"Where are you going?" Willie asked suspiciously.

"To get us a ride."

About half of the mine cars were moving at various speeds along the rails, pulled along by underground cables. Some were full of rocks; some were empty. Indy went for an empty one.

As the trolley rolled in to the central collection

terminal, Indiana ran alongside it, holding on, trying to stop it, getting half-dragged. All at once the car stopped, seemingly of its own accord.

It wasn't of its own accord.

Indy jerked to a halt and looked up to see a giant guard stopping the cart with his arm. A really giant guard. The same guard he'd tangled with twice before. He hadn't done too well either time. Okay, then, so it was a grudge match.

Indy started to throw a punch, then thought better of it. Instead, he stooped for a piece of timber and smashed the guard in the head. The timber splintered. The guard didn't move. This looked serious.

He grabbed a sledgehammer out of the truck, swung it into the giant's left ribs. The titan only smiled, belched, tore the hammer out of Indy's hand, tossed it aside. Then he wrapped his left arm around Indy's waist. Then he punched Indy's belly in.

Indy hit the dirt. He bounced right back up, kicking the giant in the face, but the colossus barely rocked. This looked really serious.

The guard seized Indy again, punched him twice in the chest, once in the throat, dragged his head along the side of the mine car, then lifted the unfortunate adventurer into the air.

Shorty lashed the big ape with Indy's fallen bullwhip. There was a CRACK and a yowl: the lummox dropped Indy into the mine car. Shorty flayed the giant again, but the brute just grabbed him and flung him far away.

The mine car started moving, pulled up a long slope by its cable. The giant jumped in. In a moment, the two men were bashing away at each other, riding up the hill.

Willie followed the cart along at a distance, sometimes watching the fight, sometimes throwing rocks at the guard (when she could get a clear shot), sometimes looking for an empty, freely moving car on a rail that didn't dead-end.

Indy had found a weak spot at the giant's neck and was doing his best to batter it with an iron bar. But every time he started pressing his advantage, horrible pain would wrack his body and he'd crumple again to the guard's pummeling.

"What's the matter with him?" Willie shouted to Short Round.

Short Round saw the problem; he pointed up. There, on the next ledge higher, stood the Maharajah. He was jabbing his turban pin into his Indiana Jones doll.

The mine car reached the top of the slope and tipped over, dumping Indy and the giant out with a pile of rocks onto a moving conveyer belt. The giant picked up a spade. Indy raised a pickax to parry, but dropped it as the agony seared through his face. He rolled over just in time to avoid being brained by the giant's blow.

On the shelf high above, the Maharajah twisted his pin in the face of the little figurine.

Willie found an empty car that appeared to lead out to one of the exit tunnels. "I got one, Indy, I got one! We can go home now!"

Indy wasn't listening, though. He was alternately dodging punches or swinging a kerosene can against the guard's head.

Shorty, meanwhile, had made his way to a thin waterfall that cascaded down from the Maharajah's level. It poured into a revolving wheel of buckets, the function of which was to bring full buckets of water up to the top tier. Shorty jumped onto a full bucket at the bottom, rode it up to the higher level, jumped off again. He ran across the ledge; moments later, he was battling the evil Prince. The doll skittered across the ground.

Indiana skittered across the conveyer belt, wrestling with the guard. He could see the end of the line now: a great iron wheel that crushed every rock and boulder that passed under its momentous turning. The conveyer fed the crusher endlessly; it was insatiable.

Willie threw rocks at the giant. The giant pounded Indy and sometimes threw rocks back at Willie. Indy kicked at the giant or blasted him with the kerosene can as Short Round struggled with the Maharajah in mortal, twelve-year-old combat. With each passing second Indy was conveyed nearer to the jaws of the stone-crusher.

Shorty got the Maharajah by the throat. The Maharajah stabbed the turban pin deeply into Short Round's leg. Shorty winced in pain, rolling away, holding his leg. This prince was more of a streetfighter than he looked. But that was fine; Short Round was no debutante.

The giant grabbed Indy's arm, but the sleeve tore off. As he twisted back off-balance, the huge man's sash got snagged by the iron roller. He desperately tried to crawl away against the relentless tugging. But it had him. He screamed hideously as his body was pulled under the crusher, feet first, and pulverized.

Bloody rock dust crunched out the other side.

Up on the high level, Short Round stumbled to a near wall, grabbed a torch; he turned as Zalim Singh rushed him with a knife. Shorty crouched and extended his arm; the Maharajah impacted himself on the burning tar.

He wailed, fell back, sat down hard. Short Round threw dirt on a flap of burning cloth, prepared to leap on the young monarch again... but there was no need.

The Maharajah looked as if he'd just awakened from a bad dream. And so he had.

Short Round sat before him. He'd seen this transformation before. "It was the black nightmare of Kali," he explained to Zalim Singh. Short Round, like The Shadow, knew what evil lurked in the hearts of some men; some boys, too.

The Maharajah nodded. His eyes were full of grief. "They made me do evil things. May Lord Krishna forgive me." It was only fragmented visions now, but they stabbed at his conscience like broken shards.

Indiana, in the meantime, had jumped up to a catwalk above the conveyor belt, leading near where Willie waited with the empty trolley. Time was running out, though. Mola Ram arrived, with reinforcements.

In seconds, they were encircling the place.

"Get down here, Shorty!" yelled Willie. "I got us a ride!"

A guard rushed her. She yanked the iron brake handle off the mine car and bashed his head in—then held another, more leery, at bay.

Short Round lowered himself down the rocky balcony. The Maharajah leaned over to see him off. "Please, listen. To go out you must take the left tunnel," he warned.

Shorty stared at him uncertainly a moment, then

knew he was telling the truth. "Thanks," he said, and scooted down the rock.

Indy was having trouble. Three guards jumped down to the catwalk, forcing him back. He shinnied up a short ladder, knocked it away, ran along a parallel ledge. The guards opened fire with pistols. Indy shielded himself behind a cart, wheeling it to the next catwalk.

Willie started her car rolling down the track; climbed in. The guard who'd been watching her took his chance now and grabbed her leg. Short Round was there, though. He picked up a perfect rock, took his stance, checked the runner at first, shouted, "Lefty Grove!" and let fly with a sliding pitch that caught the guard hard behind the ear. The man went down.

Another guard grabbed Shorty from behind as Willie's car slowly started gathering momentum. Shorty slithered out of his assailant's grip and kar-ate-kicked him in the stomach.

A wild-looking priest now began chasing Willie's truck. Shorty raced up to intersect the man, rolled into a little ball, threw himself in the attacker's path. They both went spilling in different directions. Short Round got right up again, pursued the mine car an-other fifty feet, and finally managed to jump on, just as it was really picking up speed. Willie pulled him in.

They looked around quickly until they spotted Indiana, still dodging guards up in the catwalks and scaffolds.

"Indy, come on, hurry!" they bellowed together.

Indy looked down at them, saw where he was in relation to them, saw where they were heading: into a large exit tunnel at the near end of the quarry.

He ran hard, jumping from ledge to ladder to catwalk to beam. Guards were shooting at him from all sides now, splintering wood, chipping rock. Mola Ram stood on high ground, shouting orders, pointing to the departing commandoes.

"They are escaping! Kill them!" he commanded in Hindi. The guards doubled their efforts.

Indy came to the end of the scaffolding. Guards rallied behind him; below and above. He leapt into dim air, caught hold of a block and tackle that carried him at dizzying speed, down, on a line coverging with the accelerating mine car.

"Follow them! Kill them!" Mola Ram roared.

Bullets whizzed and exploded. The car sailed on toward the tunnel; Indy sailed on toward the car. When he was a few yards above it, a few to the side, he let go—and flew, in a not-so-gentle arc, into the speeding gondola.

They whooped, crouching down to avoid the caroming bullets. Indy noticed an unconscious thug at the bottom of the car. He took the man's gun, then dumped him out over the edge, just as the car tore into the blackness of the tunnel.

Suddenly it was totally dark; no more bullets shattered the air; and they were barreling down the tracks at the bottom of the cab. And they were going to make it.

Back in the quarry, Mola Ram watched the cart zip into the first leg of the escape route to vanish from sight. Fury darkened his eye as he whispered to his aide. "They've stolen the Sankara Stones. They must be stopped."

9

Cliffhangers

Torches lighted the way for the careening trolley.
Indy quickly saw the tracks separate in two directions, one back around toward the quarry again, one
straight out. He lifted a shovel from the floor of the
car, swung it down the side just in time to hit a
switch on the tracks that hunted them, with a
CLANG, onto the exit rail.

This line soon entered another cavern, and
branched into two more. Before any action could
be taken, it tore down the right fork, into that tunnel.

Short Round looked worried. "No, Indy, big mistake. *Left* tunnel."

But it was too late. They all just held on as the
mine car shot down into the darkness of the echoing
caves.

There were long descents, short rises; Indiana

had a sense they were going even deeper into the mountain. The wind rushed past his face as he stuck his head up on the wide curves, still picking up speed. Willie huddled in the bottom of the cart, trying to catch her breath. Short Round had seen roller coasters in a couple of movies, but nothing as good as this. Except maybe the one in *King Kong*, at the end of the film, when the ape derailed it. But Short Round wasn't scared of monkeys, no matter how big: he'd been born in the Year of the Monkey—which he now took for a good sign that this ride would end well.

Back in the quarry, Mola Ram organized pursuit cars. Guards carrying Khyber rifles filled two wagons and pushed off, rolling into the tunnel the infidels had taken.

Ram stopped a third car from joining the chase, though. He had a more foolproof plan for destroying the thieves of the Sankara Stones, a plan that didn't involve losing more loyal guards in rail-to-rail combat.

Resolutely he walked toward the large side cavern where the main waterfall tumbled into the black crystal of the underground lake.

Indy reaffixed the brake handle to the front of the car, the one Willie had pulled off during the fight, and applied variable pressure to it as they hurtled around, trying to control their speed. Even so, once or twice they took a corner on two wheels. Indy scrunched down, to lower their center of gravity and prevent derailment.

Short Round peered over the back end, expecting

trouble. He'd been a thief half his life; it was second nature to him to keep an eye over his shoulder when he was running with the goods.

Willie stayed low. She could see the horizontal support beams of the tunnel racing overhead. They seemed to flash by closer to the car with each successive turn: the tunnel was getting lower.

She was about to mention this, when all at once the car plunged downward—at what felt to Willie like a vertical drop, but was probably just a rather steep incline—throwing them all against the back of the cab; leaving Willie's stomach somewhere back up in the neighborhood of the top of the grade.

They leveled out. Indy returned to the brake lever. Shorty returned to his rear-end lookout post. He was soon rewarded.

A gunshot rang out. Short Round saw the first Thugee car take a curve far behind them. On the straightaway, the riflemen began blasting.

Bullets richocheted off the back of their car, all around the tunnel. They ducked low, until the next bend. Then Indy shouted over the din of the clackering wheels.

"Shorty, come here and take the brake!"

"Read you loud and clear, Indy!" Short Round scurried forward to take the wildly vibrating handle from Indy.

Indiana slid back to the rear. "Slow on the curves," he shouted up, "or we'll fly off the tracks!"

"Read you loud and clear, Indy!" the boy shouted back. He gripped the brake with every muscle in his little hands; he grinned with every muscle in his little face.

With yet one more sinking feeling, Willie realized that this catastrophe was Short Round's idea of a good time. She yelled up at him in a panic of anger: "I hope you're better at this than driving a car!"

His grin grew even more ferocious. "We could let you off right here, lady!" She wasn't his mother *yet*.

Willie closed her eyes, counted to ten. Dear God, the child was turning into another Indiana Jones.

Mola Ram directed a detail of men to the waterfall—more precisely, to the gargantuan cistern that took the run-off from the falls. Like a great round iron pot, it rested on timber and rock supports that wedged it in place, poised there, almost delicately.

Mola Ram had his men get sledgehammers.

The lead chase car was gaining on the escaping vehicle. Indy, Willie, and Shorty spent more time crouching as rifle bullets flared in the iron-rich ore that filled the tunnels around them. Sporadically Short Round would pop up to brake on a curve; Indy would do the same to shoot. He only had six shells in his gun, though, so he was judicious in his firing.

He actually hit one rifleman, but another immediately took his place. They seemed unstoppable; they were getting closer.

At the next hard turn, Short Round rode the brake with all his weight. The brake pad screeched on the metal wheel; sparks flew like a comet tail.

The ceiling was getting lower again as well. The support beams rushed over their heads so closely, Indy could barely look over the top of the car to shoot. His last bullet buried itself in a length of timber.

One of the thugs sat up to take proper aim and

died a hero to his cause: his head struck an onrushing beam; he was knocked from the car in two directions. This lightened the load of the pursuit car considerably; it increased its speed.

Indy crouched low, his knees touching Willie's. "Get down, everybody," he barked. "Get down. They're coming."

Mola Ram's men rhythmically swung their sledgehammers against the wedges under the huge water-filled cistern. Several tons of weight pressed down, holding the struts in place. Mola Ram was not worried, though. They would give with each blow, a millimeter at a time, until they finally gave way completely.

And then the cistern would roll over, spill.

"Faster," he ordered.

The sledgehammer rhythm picked up its pace.

Indy yelled at Short Round. "Let up on the brake!"

"What!" shouted the kid. They were already hurtling along like a train in a silent movie.

"Let her go! Our only chance is outrunning them."

"What about the curves?" Willie pointed out.

"To hell with the curves." He pulled Short Round's hands off the brake. They tore around the bend half an inch airborne, then settled back down on the tracks with a thunderous rattle.

"We're going too fast!" cried Willie.

The guards in the pursuit car were thrown from side to side; they almost went over. Indy's car hit the next curve on two wheels. "Get over on the other side!"

They all hugged the inside, low, as the car whipped around.

The Thuggee car, just behind, also took the curve at full speed. They were heavier, though—big men, long guns. They derailed.

The car flew off the tracks sideways. The guards' heads peered over the top like worried fledglings. They weren't worried long, though. They crashed into a stone wall with an explosion that shook the cavern.

Indy's cart rocketed away. The second Thuggee car was pummeled with debris from the wreck; the driver grabbed for his brake, to avoid the same fate.

Indy smiled boyishly. "One down, one to go."

Mola Ram's guards continued to hammer away at the supports under the mammoth cistern. Finally one of the lateral rocks began to crumble, then quickly shattered under the redistributed pressure.

High above the workers, the cistern listed fractionally. Water lapped over the edge, sloshed around the rim, as the huge tank creaked into this new, slightly tilted position.

Indiana hefted a railroad tie out of the bottom of the car. He leaned it against the rear wall and, after the next burst of gunfire, teetered it over the back, onto the tracks.

It bounced along the rails a few seconds—long enough for the pursuers to spot it and scream, before crashing into it. They weren't demolished, though; the tie just skidded, tumbled, bounced out of the way like a large, useless matchstick.

The guards looked overjoyed. Indy looked sick.

"Any more ideas?" Willie moped. She'd largely decided to forget about getting out of this place alive. That way, maybe she'd be pleasantly surprised. It seemed pretty much out of her hands, in any case.

"Yeah. Short cut," said Indy. He swung at another set of points on the track; the car veered off into a side tunnel. A moment later, the second car forked off in a different direction and disappeared.

"Bad guys go away," noted Short Round with some suspicion. "Where they going?" It couldn't be that easy.

It wasn't. The Thuggee cart suddenly reappeared out of another tunnel—on a parallel track, directly beside them.

One of the guards fired point blank at them, but, in all the jostling, missed. Indy grabbed the muzzle of the rifle, wrenching it from the thug's hands. He swung it around, catching one guard on the jaw.

Another snatched Shorty by the arm.

"Indy, help!"

Indy grabbed his other arm. The two men had a tug-of-war with the boy while Willie jabbed at the others with the Khyber rifle.

Indy won the pulling contest; Shorty lurched into their car, falling to the bottom. In the same second, another guard leapt across onto the rear of Indy's truck. He got his arm around Indy from behind.

Indiana swiveled around and leaned back, scraping the thug against the stone wall flying by. This stunned the man enough so that Indy was able to break his grip. He whirled in a crouch, then came up punching—and knocked the guard over the end of the car.

He turned to help Willie, who'd just slammed another thug down with the gun butt. Before he took a step, the guard he'd just dispatched climbed over the back of the truck again, though; he bashed Indy on the head with a rock. Indy went down.

Willie stepped up instantly. She took aim, gave the man a good right hook to the face, and sent him sailing down onto the tracks for the count. She hadn't spent time in Shanghai without learning *something*.

Indy stood up wobbly. "My mistake." He smiled.

She handed him his hat.

In the car alongside, the guards were picking up their guns. They'd dropped behind about five yards during the last interchange.

"Get down!" shouted Indy. He saw something useful.

He grabbed the shovel, swung it hard at an overhead dumper release; then hit the deck.

A barrage of rocks, dirt, and gravel pelted both cars from the dumper. The following car took it full bore: one guard was crushed outright, then the whole trolley was derailed by debris on the tracks. They went over in a cloud of rock dust as Indy's group, bruised and dirty, roared on.

Roared on into a tunnel studded with stalactites. Indy stuck his head up, but scarcely had time to say "Duck!" The car crashed through the rocky projections, breaking off tips that hung too low from the ceiling, then careening out again with only a minimal loss of speed.

Willie looked up this time. There was once again nothing to do but close her eyes: twenty feet ahead was a break in the track.

They hit the break at sixty. The *good* news was there was a five-foot drop-off beyond it. The car went sailing over the edge, dropped the distance, landed with a CRUNCH on the lower section of track . . . and kept going.

Willie giggled lightly. Anything goes.

* * *

The sledgehammers kept beating. Two more rock supports gave way; then a third. Almost in slow motion, the enormous pot began to tip.

There were shouts as the guards ran for cover.

Mola Ram stood, removed, on a platform overlooking the event. The noise alone was incredible—the sound of the earth's own engines—as the huge vessel rolled, keeled over, crashed to its side.

With a deafening roar, a million gallons of water burst across the cavern in a surging tidal wave.

Into the tunnels.

This new length of track was straight; the tunnel, high.

Indy smiled with that air of nonchalance Willie both loved and hated. "Brake, Shorty, brake," he said.

Short Round was a little sorry the ride was over already, but figured there'd be other rides. He pulled casually on the brake lever.

It didn't work.

He pulled harder.

It came off in his hands.

"Oh, oh. Big mistake," he said, wide-eyed.

Willie only nodded. "Figures."

It also figured that they were just heading into a long, gentle slope that didn't seem to go anywhere but down.

They, of course, began moving faster still.

Indy bent over the front of the car to look underneath. The entire braking apparatus was hanging loose from the pad. Indiana pulled himself back in.

The three of them looked at each other with complete understanding of what had to be done. They'd been through a lot together. Here was half a moment to remember it.

Willie thought: *You're a good man, Indiana Jones. Wish I'd known you somewhere else.*

Indy thought: *Hope you two guys stick together, 'cause I sure haven't been much help to either one of you.*

Shorty thought: *If this lady is the last treasure Chao-pao discovered before he leaves me in this life, she must be pretty big fine treasure. Better I keep her.*

Willie and Shorty each squeezed one of Indy's hands. Then Indy climbed out over the front of the racing car.

Facing backwards, he lowered himself down. Willie and Short Round held on to his arms and jacket, to give him extra bracing. When his bottom was inches from the rails, he swung a leg underneath the car, trying to kick at the brake pad. The ground was a blur beneath him. His feet fell momentarily— he bumped along, in danger of being dragged under the iron wheels—but he regained his grip.

With one leg he managed to find a foothold on the undercarriage of the car; with his other, he located the brake pad. Slowly, firmly, he applied pressure with his foot; the pad closed against the spinning disk.

"We're going too fast," noted Willie with a feverish grin. She was sweating; her hands were cramping, holding on to Indy for all of their dear lives.

Then she looked up, for one last laugh: the tunnel was ending; the tracks stopped dead at a not too distant stone wall.

Shorty saw it too. "We're gonna crash!" he shouted. The ride was not supposed to end this way at all.

Indiana looked around behind him. No doubt about it: they were flying at top speed into a wall the size of a mountain, and the first thing to hit was going to be Indiana Jones.

He slammed his foot into the brake pad with every ounce of strength he could muster. The pad screamed against the angry iron. Sparks shot out in skyrockets. Indiana's sole was getting hotter, but he closed his mind to the pain, concentrated only on the force his leg could exert, didn't waste energy thinking about the wall.

The wall drew nearer.

But not quite as quickly. Indy groaned with pushing; the brake pad began to smoke. The car slowed even further. The wall approached. Indy jammed down with his whole body. The car slowed more. Indy pressed.

It slowed until it ran down the last few yards to the dead end; rolled gently to a stop, and just nudged Indy's back against the wall.

He stood, limped a few steps away, his boot smoking. "Water," he rasped.

The others got out of the cab, stood there shakily, smiling tentatively.

They could see that the tunnel continued on, somewhat to the left, without any more tracks. So they started to walk.

No one spoke. They were all too full of what had just happened.

Soon, a wind rose quickly to a stiff blow. Then a strange rumbling sound echoed down the tunnel from behind. The walls seemed to be reverberating.

It felt . . . worrisome.

They exchanged uncertain looks, shrugged, walked a little faster. The wind, in particular, disturbed Indy. There shouldn't be so high a wind so low in the earth.

The noise grew louder. They glanced over their shoulders. Nothing. "Indy?" said Willie.

He wasn't sure, but he grasped Willie by the hand; all three of them started jogging.

The rumbling increased. Small debris began to fall from the ceiling; the ground was almost quaking. It made Short Round remember a volcano movie he didn't want to remember just now. He wondered if The Lord of Thunder was angry about something.

They ran. Ran fast, though they didn't know why. Yet.

The noise was stunning now. Willie looked around again. Suddenly she slowed; stopped. Stopped dead in mid-stride, paralyzed with disbelief, awe. Doom.

It was a monster wall of water, crashing spectacularly into the opposite embankment of a cross tunnel far behind them.

But not far enough.

Willie whispered. "Oh, shit."

Short Round and Indiana stopped to see what was keeping Willie. What they saw was a watery cataclysm spewing forward, soon to overtake them. For a long moment, they just stared.

Then Indy grabbed Willie, and they all ran like hell.

The tidal wave smashed furiously down, booming closer every second. At its foaming muzzle it carried the debris of a hundred cluttered tunnels: boulders, branches, animals.

They weren't going to make it.

Except just maybe, at that small side tunnel in the bend ahead...

"There!" Indy screamed above the roar. "Dive!"

They sprang toward the hole. Short Round dove through first, just like stealing home. Indy shoved Willie in, then followed himself—just as the tsunami exploded past in the main shaft.

This narrow tunnel dropped precipitously. They slid at a tumble, showered by the small side current of water diverted from the central stream.

They rolled down the chute to a larger tunnel. Shorty looked particularly lighthearted. "That was fun. Wait a minute, I do it again."

Indy collared him before he could take a step, however, pointing him in a more proper direction. Where did these kids learn this stuff? he wondered.

The growl of the tidal wave receded as they caught their breath.

Up ahead, Willie dared to believe she could actually see light, yes, at the end of the tunnel. She was about to mention it when a new explosion boomed behind them. They turned to see another arm of the same wave cascading down now this tunnel, with an alarming force.

They all hollered in unison, started running full tilt toward the daylight. The towering wall of water surged mirthlessly after them.

They raced to the mouth of the tunnel; the first tongues of water were on their backs. Out into sunshine, they emerged...

And teetered on the brink. The tunnel exited midway up a cliff: they were looking at a three-hundred-foot sheer drop straight down to a rocky gorge.

Arms flailing to keep their balance, they hovered

there a lifetime. Then Indy swung Willie to a narrow ledge on one side of the tunnel-mouth cliff-face, pushing Short Round after her; he jumped to the other side—just as the tidal wave crashed between them, out this gutterspout in the rock. At the forefront was the wreckage: rail ties shot out, and barrels, and all manner of detritus; even a mine car rocketed past. All surging in the water.

It was a massive gusher, spurting out of this and multiple other tunnels all around them in the cliffside. Short Round and Willie stayed balanced on their little ledge; Indy remained perched on his, on the opposite side of the erupting geyser.

Willie looked down for a second, but vertigo nearly overcame her. Water thundered into the gorge below; crocodiles slithered angrily in the shallow streambed there, disturbed out of their afternoon slumber.

Indy looked around. The gorge was maybe a hundred yards across; craggy bluffs rose on the other side to an expanse of flat plain that resembled the way home, as far as Indy could tell from this distance. Then he saw the bridge.

It was a thin rope bridge, swinging between the two plateaus. On this side it emerged about twenty feet above and another twenty beyond where Willie and Shorty were clutching the rocks. Indiana shouted to them across the blasting waterspout.

"Willie, head for the bridge!" He pointed up.

She looked. She looked away. Would this never end?

"Nothing to it," Short Round encouraged. "Follow me."

He edged along the narrow precipice on which

they were balanced, toward the outcropping that lay directly beneath the bridge. Reluctantly, Willie followed. Once under the bridge, they began climbing up the rocks.

Rockclimbing is an activity at which twelve-year-olds are known to excel; this instance was exemplary of that fact. Short Round scrabbled like a mountain goat, finding nooks and handholds that seemed to have been awaiting his arrival all these centuries. Willie was somewhat less agile in this endeavor. Still, she was a dancer; moreover, she was running for her life—and she hadn't gotten as far as she *had* gotten without being light on her feet. So she wasn't all that far behind Shorty.

Indiana was having a bit more difficulty. For one thing, his foot was still painfully numb from braking the runaway mine car. For another, he had to scale the cliff up, over, and around the several geysers between him and the bridge. The rockface here was wet, slippery, perilous.

He grabbed at the sparse scrubbrush for support; he inched along, crab-wise, slowly. With one unfeeling foot, his size was a distinct disadvantage.

Willie and Short Round pulled themselves up at the end of the bridge. Behind them in the cliff, a dark tunnel ran back into the mines. In front of them, the rope bridge looked more like taunt than hope.

It spanned the gorge like the last strands of a spiderweb at the end of the summer. It was at least a century old. It had not been built by the army corps of engineers.

It consisted of two thick lines at its base, connected by hundreds of worm-eaten, moldy wooden slats—and hundreds of empty spaces where slats used to be. Along the length of this catwalk, vertical side ropes linked the foot-span to two thin upper ropes that crossed the gorge, constituting flimsy hand railings.

Willie balked.

Short Round, though, it should be remembered, had had lots of experience running hell-bent along Shanghai rooftops, not to mention scatting across the clotheslines that connected tenement windows, to elude pursuit. So he was less deterred by the sight that confronted them now.

Tentatively, he stepped out onto the bridge. It held. He turned, smiling to Willie. "Easy like pie! Kid's stuff!"

Suddenly the board under him broke. Disintegrated, actually. Had Willie not been expecting such an eventuality, the boy would have tumbled into the abyss. But she grabbed him by the scruff, yanked him back to safety.

He looked a little pale, less cocky now. Yet there was nowhere to go but onward. Once more, he stepped onto the risky footing, concentrating very hard on being much more yin than yang. This time, it held. After weighing the alternatives, Willie followed. She tried to imagine this was a solo performance for a big producer: there could be no wrong moves; there was no starting over.

Cautiously, step by step, they made their way along the span, walking gingerly over the missing or obviously rotten slats. They had to cling to the rope hand rails, too, for the bridge swayed constantly in the wind, as well as bouncing up and down in synchronized resonance to their footfalls. Short

Round begged Madame Wind, Feng-p'o, to go play somewhere else.

It was the longest, slowest promenade Willie had ever taken.

Behind them, Indy finally pulled himself up from under the bridge. Almost free. He paused for a moment, catching his breath. Willie and Short Round, he could see, were halfway across, wavering every step. Maybe he ought to wait until they were over so his additional weight didn't rock the crossing too much.

Behind him, there were footsteps. He ducked to the side of the tunnel mouth, disengaging his whip from his belt as he did so. All at once, two Thuggee guards rushed out.

Indy cracked the whip, catching the first guard around the neck. He spilled forward, tripping the second guard. As the first Thug tried to stand, Indy kicked him in the head.

The second man stood, swinging his sword. Indy ducked and came up with his fist in the assailant's belly. The guard doubled over as Indy dove for the unconscious man's saber. Then Indy rolled to avoid a downthrust from the recovering guard's blade. He stood quickly; the two men faced each other, ready to duel.

Indy suddenly realized he didn't know a thing about this kind of sword. He hefted the flat, curved blade, held it out, up, over, trying to decide the best way to use it, when the enraged Thuggee guard shouted and charged.

Indy decided quickly that shouting was the way to go, so he made his own rather voluble, inarticulate noise and raised his scimitar to parry the attacker's first slash.

The duel was on. Sparks erupted with each CLANG as the Thuggee swordsman lunged and feinted, and lunged again. Indy's moves were more in the nature of blocks and flails, and then blocks and tackles: Indy took his opponent flying at the waist: the two of them rolled, *corps à corps*, along the rocky slope.

Indy came out on top when the tumble ended in some scrub. He punched the guard once with the iron knuckles of the swordhandle, and the fight was over.

He rose, ran back to the bridge, keeping the saber. Willie and Short Round were just about across. Indiana started out onto the rickety span.

He walked quickly, hanging on to the twine rails. Every few steps his boot would break through; he'd have to catch himself on these upper ropes. Consequently, he kept his eyes turned downward most of the way, looking to step over the weak boards. When he was nearing the middle, he heard shouting ahead. He looked up to see temple guards appear at the far end of the bridge.

Willie and Short Round were caught as soon as they stepped onto hard ground. They struggled with their captors, but it was futile. There were too many.

Indy paused, uncertain what to do next. Suddenly Willie called. "Indy, look out behind you!"

Indy turned. More guards rushed out of the tunnel behind him. He turned again. Two of the Thugs who'd captured Willie and Shorty were stepping onto the bridge ahead of him.

Indiana stood helpless in the center of the swaying bridge, with guards approaching from both sides, nothing but the crocodile-infested, rocky gorge far below, and the glorious heavens above.

Well, almost helpless. This was, after all, Indiana Jones.

The wind came up like an omen. Mola Ram, the High Priest, appeared on the far end of the bridge. He stood there in his priestly robes, smiling the smile of the man who holds all the cards. Beside him, Willie and Short Round were held fast by guards.

Indy staggered unsteadily in the buffeting wind. Bracing himself on the rope rails, he shouted to Ram. "Let my friends go!"

Mola Ram yelled to his men in Hindi. They started moving toward Indy from both sides of the bridge.

"That's far enough!" Indiana commanded.

"You are in no position to give orders, Dr. Jones," the High Priest remarked.

Indy pointed to the bag over his shoulder. "You want the stones, let them go and call off your guards! Or I'll drop the stones!"

"Drop them, Dr. Jones," said Mola Ram. "They will be easily found. But you won't!" He called out to his henchmen: "Yanne!"—and made a short hand-motion. They moved farther along the swaying bridge, closer to the madman in the middle.

Why is nothing easy? Indy wondered. Without further warning, he swung the sword he still held, cutting halfway through one of the bottom rope spans. The bridge reeled violently under the assault; the partially severed rope frayed, fiber by fiber, under the tension. The guards all stopped in their tracks.

Mola Ram nodded appreciatively. "Impressive, Dr. Jones," he congratulated his adversary. "But I don't believe you would kill yourself." He motioned again. Somewhat more reluctant now, his guards stepped farther onto the bridge, moving closer to Indy from both ends.

Indy slashed his blade again, this time into the opposing lower rope span. It, too, partly severed, continued fraying slowly: slow, like an alarm clock.

The bridge jolted; again, the guards stopped, swaying, with Indy, in the jostling wind.

Mola Ram lost his smile. He shoved Willie and Short Round out onto the bridge, then followed with his dagger drawn. He put the knife to Willie's back. "Your friends will die with you!" he bellowed.

Indiana looked at the guards in front and behind. He looked at Willie and Short Round ten feet out on the bridge, and at Mola Ram standing determined, at their backs. He looked at the land; he looked at the sky. And he shouted to all, in a voice meant to leave no doubt: "Then I guess we're all going to take a big dive!"

Indy's eyes met Short Round's. Much transpired in that meeting: memories, regrets, promises, graces; and a real clear message: this ain't no joke.

Willie saw it too. She looked wistfully at Indy: it might have been different, chum. She looked anxiously at Short Round . . . and noticed he was surreptitiously wrapping his foot around a loose rope support. Petrified—but also excited—Willie secretly did the same, twining an arm around one of the ropes as well.

Mola Ram roared like an angry priest: "Give me the stones!"

"Mola Ram," called Indiana, "you're about to meet Kali—in Hell!"

He swung the sword defiantly down. It swooshed through the air, then cut cleanly through top and bottom ropes on one side of the bridge.

Two guards fell off immediately, screaming all the way to their deaths. The rest began to flee in panic. Not quickly enough, though, for Indy slashed his sword down the other side, cleaving the span completely in two. The two halves separated, seemed to hang suspended in midair for a long, strange moment . . . and then fell apart.

Guards wailed horribly as they plunged three hundred feet to the valley. All tried desperately to cling to the remnants of rope bridge that were falling back to the cliffs; only some made it.

On the side that Indy was holding on to, three guards fell away in the first lurch. By the time the bridge finally crashed into the side of the cliff wall from which it now continued to dangle, only six people remained, grasping the fragile rope and slats: Mola Ram at the top, just several feet below the cliff-edge to which the bridge was attached; below him a guard; Willie; Short Round; another guard; and, at the very bottom, swinging precariously in space beyond an outswelling of rock, Indiana.

Willie and Shorty clung to their established footholds in the now vertical bridge. Everyone was motionless for a few seconds, realizing they were still among the living, swaying slightly, waiting to see if the ropes would hold, or settle.

Then Mola Ram began to climb. He reached very near the moorings of the rope ladder, when he grabbed a dry-rotted rung, which splintered in two. He skittered down ten feet, coming to rest finally between Willie and Short Round. In the process, he knocked off one of the guards, who fell past them all to the depth of the gully.

The ladder swung. Nobody moved.

Then Indy began to climb. He climbed past the guard, whose eyes and hands were tightly closed; he grabbed at Mola Ram's legs, to try to throw the fanatic to his death. Ram kicked him in the face, though, and resumed his own ascent.

Indy went up after him, got his foot again. He jerked hard. Mola Ram lost his grip, crashing down to Indy's level. They clutched each other and the ropes, nearly deranged with hatred. There they did battle.

Indy butted Ram in the chin with his head. Ram kneed Indy, then elbowed his neck back, then reached for his chest.

From above, Willie screamed, "Oh, my God! Indy, cover your heart!"

With sudden cold terror, Indy looked down to see Mola Ram's hand starting to enter his chest—as he'd watched the priest once do to the sacrificial victim.

He grappled with Ram's wrist, desperately holding the probing hand at bay. But slowly, fiendishly, the sorcerer's fingers began to inch through Indy's skin—into his body.

It was an icy, nauseating feeling. Not painful, really, just horribly violating his innermost spirit. It was rapacious, vile, lacerating. It made his forehead sweat; iridescent spots fluttered before his eyes. He swooned, almost fell.

But his sense of self-preservation was strong; he kept his nerve, and he forced Ram's piercing fingers away from his heart, pushed them out of his chest. Knocked the hand back against Ram's own face.

Furious, the High Priest climbed once more, while Indy took a moment to recuperate. Ram climbed only a few feet, though, to the level of his own last

207

guard. He got an arm around the man's throat, dislodged him from the ropes, and cast him down upon Indiana, in an attempt to knock Indy from the dangling ladder.

Willie and Shorty, near the top, shouted in unison. "Look out, Indy!"

The falling guard hit him square across the shoulders. Indy clung tightly; the hapless guard bounced, fell end over end, screaming all the way to his Maker.

Mola Ram laughed.

There were noises from across the gorge. Indy looked over to see a dozen more Thuggee guards streaming out of the tunnel on the other side, stranded there for lack of a bridge.

Mola Ram's voice sailed across the chasm to his men: "Kill them! Shoot them!"

The Thuggees ran up a path to a small grove of trees on a plateau above where the crossing had been. They unslung bows and arrows and took up firing positions.

Indy pulled himself higher, managing to grab on to the bottom of the High Priest's robe. Arrows began hitting all around him, though; one buried itself in the rung he was hanging on, grazing his hand. He had to let go of Ram.

Mola Ram took the opportunity to clamber up a few more steps. Shorty and Willie were waiting for him this time, however: they stomped on his hands as soon as he reached the slat they balanced on.

He let go, and fell.

Fell on top of Indy, breaking *him* loose of his hold. The two of them toppled another ten feet before catching on one of the bottom rungs.

Indy held on by his hands only. Ram didn't waste any more time struggling with the infidel. Priestly duties had not prepared him for such acrobatics; he was beginning to tire. He just wanted to get to safety.

Pushing off from Indy's head, he once again started his ascent.

Shorty finally made it to the top. He heaved himself up onto rocky ground, then turned and gave Willie a hand. They lay there panting a moment, hugging the earth, while arrows continued to fly all around them. Fortunately, all the guards on this side of the gorge had taken the plunge, so for the moment, at least, dodging arrows was all they had to worry about.

That wasn't all Indiana had to worry about. He started to mount the rope ladder yet again, when his wounded hand cramped. He crooked one elbow over a rung and for a few seconds just oscillated in the breeze. What a way to earn a living.

Indy got that old sinking feeling. Across the canyon he could see the dozen archers loosing volleys of shafts toward him. He looked down. The frayed ropes released another lower slat, which flipped in the wind like a broken propeller. It took a long time to spiral all the way to the base of the cliff.

Resolutely, Indiana renewed his climb.

Mola Ram reached the top. He extended a hand over the edge, feeling for a stable hold . . . and Willie smashed his fingers with the meanest rock she could find.

The High Priest yelped in pain, slipping out of control down the ropes, until he was once again stopped by Indiana's bulky form. They locked grips there, punching and wrestling and pivoting in the void.

On the cliff ledge above, Short Round and Willie watched the combatants powerlessly. Off to the right,

Short Round heard a noise. He tensed, ready to run or fight.

"Willie, look!" he shouted.

She followed his gaze. There, horses were galloping through a narrow pass toward them. The British cavalry was returning.

"Well, come on. It's about time," she fumed.

Captain Blumburtt and the first troops drew up their horses, dismounting quickly. A fusillade of arrows forced everyone to take cover, but they immediately leveled their long rifles at the Thuggees across the gorge, and returned fire.

Willie and Short Round crawled back to the edge, to see if they could give Indy any help.

Indy and the priest were clearly in a death struggle now. They seemed to be giving no thought to the barrage of arrows or the danger of the swinging ropes. Their only concern was to destroy each other.

Indy slugged; Ram gouged. The bag holding the stones broke loose from Indy's shoulder. He held on to the strap; but Mola Ram, remembering his treasure, grabbed the bag itself.

"No, the stones are mine!" charged the High Priest.

Indy uttered fiercely, "You have betrayed Shiva." Then, his face just inches from Mola Ram's, he began to chant Sankara's warning in Hindi, over and over: "Shive ke vishwas kate ho. Vishwas kate ho. Vishwas kate ho."

And then a remarkable thing happened. As Indy repeated the magical words, the stones began to glow through the bag.

They were painfully bright; they burned through the sack. They started falling.

Desperately, Mola Ram reached for them.

Indy kept pronouncing the incantation: "Vishnu kate ho. Vishwas kate ho."

Ram caught one of the stones, but it burned intensely hot now, searing his hand. He dropped it, letting go with his other hand as well. Indy snatched the radiant Stone out of midair as Ram released it. But to Indiana's hand, it felt cool.

For a protracted instant their eyes made contact—these last two cliffhangers—and Mola Ram looked, to Indy, as if he'd just awakened from a nightmare. Though it was a nightmare Indiana remembered only dimly, its images would haunt him forever. He felt a pang of sympathy for Mola Ram, who was balanced on the cusp of awareness of both worlds, with no future, and memories of his past sodden with horror.

The High Priest tipped backwards, his hand savagely burned. His feet broke through the splintered rung he'd been bobbling on; he pitched over, soaring down in his robes like a runaway kite, crunching at last into the jagged rocks at the bottom.

The crocodiles rapidly tore apart his lifeless corpse. Their hunger knew nothing of his abominations.

Two of the Sankara Stones hit the shallow water, sank into the murky current, and were carried downriver...somewhere.

And then there was one.

Indy put the last Sankara Stone, now dark again, into his pocket. He climbed up the hanging bridge to the top, where he was pulled over the edge by Willie, Shorty, and Blumburtt.

Across the gorge, more British troops emerged

from the mine tunnels to subdue the remaining Thuggee guards on that side. At their rear, the young Maharajah came out with the soldiers. He saw Short Round, standing with Indy; he bowed from across the chasm, to thank Shorty for saving him from the black nightmares of his own soul.

Short Round waved his cap at the Maharajah, returning the salute in thanks for bringing back the troops. The prince was obviously a born relief pitcher.

Willie stood at the lip of the gorge, looking down into the river far below. "I guess Mola Ram got what he wanted."

"Not quite," said Indy. He pulled the coveted object out of his pocket. "The last Sankara Stone."

Willie took it carefully from Indiana. She held it up to the sun. It sparkled and flashed from deep within its core, like a thing of the earth, with a secret heart.

For just a moment, they all shared its secret.

They rested a few days at the palace. The army collected many of the children, still hiding in the woods nearby, and fed them and tended their injuries. When all were strong enough to travel, Blumburtt sent a small contingent of soldiers, with Willie, Indy, and Shorty, to take the children home.

Short Round felt like King of the Children. He spent his time with them being fatherly, instructive, responsible.

He taught them never to steal, as Mola Ram had stolen them. (Except to steal bases.)

He instructed them to keep the Stars of Happiness, of Dignities, and of Longevity always near their hearts.

He taught them how to hit and pitch—with sticks and fruits.

He taught them how to distinguish mummies from draculas, and how to flip a coin, and how to look tough, but still be nice.

He sent them to Willie for tutorials in how to cloud men's minds.

He taught them the names of all the important deities, who had always responded to his prayers—though by this time, Short Round had made so many promises to so many gods, he had his doubt about any of them answering him in the future.

But Indy had answered; Indy was here. And Indy was still taking him to America.

Willie spent the time in a daze. She'd never been through anything like this before. Now that it was over, she couldn't quite believe it was over. She kept touching trees, touching Short Round, touching Indy, to make sure that it was real, that it wasn't a dream. It was still a little hard to tell.

Indy was somewhat disgruntled about losing two of the Sankara Stones—he'd held them in his hands!—but he had one. This one was his, for the time being. Besides, the children were free; that was the main thing. And the Thuggee were once again extinct.

Two days later, the troops dropped off one bunch of kids outside Mayapore village, then went on to escort the remainder to other outlying towns.

Indiana and his companions walked back down the dirt road into Mayapore, followed by the village's youngsters. They were astonished to view the landscape: what had been barren countryside was being reborn.

Trees budded beside streams that flowed clear

and vital. Flowers were trying to bloom; the hills had turned from brown to green. Peasants were tilling the fields.

In the village itself, people were rebuilding their primitive dwellings. Fine crafts hung from the walls; the villagers worked on the details of their lives with a vigor that spread to all the land.

Shouts of joy arose as the peasants saw their own returning. They dropped what they were doing and ran out to meet the children, who rushed on ahead to this jubilant reunion.

There were tears, and laughter, and all manner of grateful tidings. The shaman approached Indiana, touched his fingers to his forehead, bowed. The three travelers returned his greeting.

He was profoundly moved as he spoke to Indy. "We know you are coming back"—he indicated the surrounding landscape—"when life returns to our village."

Willie nodded. "I've never seen a miracle before." But this was a miracle, plain and simple. It made her grin brightly. Miracles not only *could* happen; they sometimes *did*.

The shaman smiled. "Now you see the magic of the 'rock' you bring back."

Indy took the stone from his pocket, unwrapped it from the bit of Sankara cloth he still had. "Yes, I've seen its power."

The shaman reverently took the stone from Indy, bowed to them again; then walked, with the other elders, to the sacred shrine. Willie, Indy, and Shorty stayed back.

The shaman knelt before the small altar, placed the Sankara Stone in its niche, chanted: "Om sivaya namah om..."

Indy and Willie walked away.

"You could've kept it," she said to him.

"What for? They'd put it in a museum, where it'd be another rock collecting dust."

"It would've gotten you your fortune and glory."

Indy shrugged, then smiled slyly. "Well, it's a long way to Delhi. Anything could still happen."

She looked at him as if he were crazy. "Oh, no. No, thanks. No more adventures for me, Dr. Jones."

"Sweetheart, after all the fun we've had..."

A big purple cloud began welling up inside her. What was he, nuts? They were alive—quite accidentally, she thought. Wasn't that good enough for him? Fuming, frustrated ire rose in her craw.

"If you think I'd go with you to Delhi or anyplace else after all the trouble you've gotten me into, think again, buster," she started, and then she got rolling. "I'm going home to Missouri, where they never ever feed you snake before ripping your heart out and lowering you into hot pits. This is not my idea of a swell time! No more Anything Goes! No more—"

She stopped before she started frothing; turned, walked toward a villager with a bundle on his back. "Excuse me, sir?" she called to him. "I need a guide to Delhi. I'm really very good on an elephant."

The whip cracked, wrapping around Willie's waist. With a gentle insistence, Indy pulled her in to his arms.

She resisted only briefly. No use fighting karma: this clinch was meant to be since the second he'd walked into the club, and their eyes had closed the deal.

They kissed.

It was warm, glad, giving as a summer rain.

Water rained down on them in a brief, torrential

shower. They separated, looked up. There was Short Round, sitting on the back of his baby elephant, which was spraying them gleefully with its trunk.

Short Round laughed. Indy and Willie laughed. The baby elephant laughed.

"Very funny," said Short Round. "Very funny big joke."

They did eventually all make it to America. But that is another story.